The *Tablet*

Journeys to
FAYRAH

The Portal is also available as a Drama on Tape at your local bookstore.

The Tablet

Bill Myers

BETHANY HOUSE PUBLISHERS
MINNEAPOLIS, MINNESOTA 55438

Published by Bethany House Publishers
A Ministry of Bethany Fellowship, Inc.
6820 Auto Club Road, Minneapolis, Minnesota 55438

Printed in the United States of America

Library of Congress Cataloging-in-Publication Data

Myers, Bill, 1953–
    The tablet / Bill Myers.
       p. cm. — (Journeys to Fayrah ; bk. 4)
    Summary: Cross-dimensionalized once more to the land of
Fayrah. Denise and Nathan continue in their spiritual discoveries
as they make minor wrong choices and fail to trust the powerful
and loving Imager.

    [1. Fantasy. 2. Christian life—Fiction.] I. Title. II. Series:
Myers, Bill, 1953–   Journeys to Fayrah ; bk. 4.
PZ7.M9823Tab   1992
[Fic]—dc20   92-34301
ISBN 1–55661–299–0   CIP
                                 AC

For Dale Evrist . . .

a man of truth, commitment and integrity.

CONTENTS

— Chapter One —

The Signal

"DENNNYYYYYY . . ."

Denise Wolff tossed and turned in the chair beside her mom's hospital bed. For the third time that night she dreamed of how her mother had fallen off the ladder. For the third time that night she saw her tumbling like a Barbie doll from their second-story window. And for the third time that night she heard the crack of shrubs and the sickening thud of her mother hitting the ground.

"Mom. . . . MOM!"

No answer.

Denise raced toward the bushes, a cold knot already forming in her stomach. "MOTHER!"

She found her mom sprawled out on the ground, trying to catch her breath. "I'm all right, Denny," she gasped. "I'm all right, it's OK."

But it wasn't OK. Denise could see that in a second. It wasn't OK the way her mom kept trying to breathe but couldn't. And it wasn't OK the way one of her legs was twisted and pointed in the wrong direction.

Denny's mom had been trying to change the storm windows, as she did every spring. Of course, if there were a husband around the house, she wouldn't have had to. Then again, if there were a husband around, they'd probably have enough money to buy windows that didn't need changing.

But her mom had no husband—at least not any-more. And Denny had no father—at least not one she could remember. He'd left when she was four.

Now it was just the two of them—mother and daughter. Oh sure, they had their fights—especially when it came to the torn and baggy clothes Denny always wore. But the two loved each other fiercely. And when the chips were down, they always knew the other would be there.

And that afternoon "being there" meant Denise calling 911, riding with her mom in the ambulance, pacing in the waiting room, and listening to the doc-tors say she had some bruised ribs and a shattered leg.

Of course, everybody told Denise to go home and get some rest. "Your mother will be fine," they said. "She's under mild sedation—she'll barely know you're here."

But Denny wouldn't listen. She wouldn't leave. She'd already lost one parent; she wasn't about to lose another. Instead, she grabbed a blanket, borrowed a pillow, and tried to get comfortable in the steel and vinyl chair next to her mom's bed.

Here she waited. And here her world famous anger started to burn. . . .

Why had her mom fallen?
Why did things always go wrong?
Why was life always so hard?

Of course, Denny knew Imager loved her. After all, she'd been to Fayrah. She'd even been re-Breathed. But sometimes that love seemed so far away. Sometimes it seemed as if Imager had forgotten, or that he didn't know, or, worse yet, that he simply didn't care.

"It would be a whole lot different if I were in charge," she muttered as she drifted in and out of her fitful sleep. "A *whole* lot different."

The thought churned in her mind. The thought of being in charge, the thought of replacing Imager, the thought of being the boss.

Unfortunately, she had no idea that the thought would trigger a little alarm—a little alarm for a creature who had sworn revenge upon her—a creature on the molten, hot surface of Ecknolb. . . .

———

"TeeBolt! Come quickly!" cried the Merchant of Emotions. "It's happening, it's happening!" The Merchant turned from his monitors and chuckled as he watched the huge, hairy TeeBolt gallop toward him. The animal's six furry legs raced across the steaming rocks as fast as they could carry him. He would have barked in pain, but he had nothing to bark with. In an outburst of anger the Merchant had destroyed TeeBolt's voice epochs ago.

"Look, my pet, it's the Denise—the creature who destroyed our dear Illusionist!" The Merchant of Emotions threw his claws up in joy. He fluttered his wings in delight. The Illusionist had been his sister—until Denise accidentally destroyed her in the Sea of Mirrors. Ever since then, the Merchant had vowed vengeance. Not only upon Denny, but upon all of her kind, upon all Upside-Downers. The only problem was, he had been confined to the desolate planet of Ecknolb, forbidden ever to enter the Upside-down Kingdom—at least on his own. At least without an invitation.

But all that was changing. For months he'd been monitoring Denise's thoughts, waiting for the opportunity. Now it was here . . . the beginning of distrust, the seed of rebellion. "The Denise is doubting!" the Merchant chortled with excitement. "What a fool. The Denise thinks it knows more than Imager!"

Of course, TeeBolt had no idea what his master was talking about or why he was so excited. But it made little difference. The Merchant simply glanced down to the Emotion Generator strapped to his chest, scanned the dozens of silver switches, and flipped the one labeled EXCITEMENT. A cloud of mist shot from a nozzle on the contraption. It struck TeeBolt dead center and filled him with so much EXCITEMENT he couldn't contain himself. He was so thrilled that he began leaping on the Merchant and panting. The only trouble was that when he panted he drooled.

"Get down you, you nincompoop! Stop that slobbering!"

Immediately TeeBolt hopped down and closed his mouth. For if he didn't hop down and close his mouth, he might not have anything to hop down with or have a mouth to close.

"Now if I can just get the Denise to dream about the Tablet—if I can just convince the Denise to begin writing on it." The Merchant spun back to the monitor and adjusted several dials. "Then the Denise will invite us to her world. Then I can get my claws on the

Tablet. And then," he began to grin, "then we can finally destroy her wretched little world."

The Merchant broke into laughter. The joy of destroying Imager's precious Upside-down Kingdom caused every crystal scale on his body to quiver with delight. TeeBolt was still too overwhelmed with EXCITEMENT to understand the humor . . . until the Merchant reached down and snapped on the LAUGHTER switch.

Another cloud of mist shot out and struck TeeBolt. The animal began to laugh uncontrollably. He couldn't help himself. That was the power the Merchant of Emotions had over TeeBolt—over all creatures who gave him control. And because of this power, he had been banned from the Upside-down Kingdom.

But even from great distances he could sometimes direct dreams. Not a lot, mind you. But if the dreamer was angry enough, if there was enough rebellion in their hearts, then there might be room for the Merchant to move in. He might be able to nudge a dream or two their way. He might be able to influence their thoughts ever so slightly.

That's exactly what he would do with Denise. . . .

That's exactly how he hoped to enter and destroy her world.

———

Back in Grandpa O'Brien's Secondhand Shop, Joshua and Nathan were arguing again. Like Denise, they'd both visited Fayrah. They'd both been re-Breathed. And they'd both started to grow in Imager's ways. But when it came to good old-fashioned brotherly bickering . . . well, these guys were pros.

"You're the oldest," Nathan whined.

"So?"

"So, till Grandpa gets back from deliveries, *let me* visit Denny and *you* stay to look after the shop."

"No way," Josh argued as he stopped to adjust his hair in the reflection of a used toaster. "All you and Denny ever do is fight. She needs me at the hospital— somebody more mature, more sensitive to look after her."

"Oh, please," Nathan groaned. "I think I'm going to get sick." He turned and limped toward the counter. His hip, the one that had bothered him since birth, was acting up again. But he wouldn't let his brother see the pain. No way. Not when he had an argument to win.

They'd been going around like this ever since Denise phoned from the hospital, and they still hadn't reached an agreement. You see, the only person more stubborn than Nathan was Joshua. And the only person more stubborn than Joshua was Nathan. Sound impossible? It was, and that was the problem.

Luckily, the standoff was about to end. For suddenly they heard a very familiar voice:

Now come on little buddies,
don't get in a tither
Put aside all yer fighting,
and let us draw hither.

The boys looked at each other. Only one person in the universe had such awful poetry. "Aristophenix!" they shouted. "Aristophenix, where are you?"

Next came the familiar:

Beep . . .
Bop . . .
Burp . . .
Bleep . . .

of the three very good friends cross-dimensionalizing into their world.

And then . . .

"GET US DOWN—GET US DOWN FROM HERE!"

The brothers snapped their heads back to see Aristophenix, a roly-poly creature with checkered vest and walking stick, and Listro Q, a tall purple dude in a tuxedo, spinning high above their heads. Apparently Listro Q's aim with the Cross-Dimensionalizer hadn't improved much. He and Aristophenix were caught on the ceiling fan, spinning round and round and round.

"Won't you—*WHOA*—ever get—*WHOO*—the hang of that thing?" Aristophenix cried.

"Cool, it is," Listro Q shouted. "Any day now, of it I'm sure."

The third member of the party wasn't caught on the fan. He was darting about their heads chattering a mile a minute. Or was he laughing? It was hard to tell with Samson. The part ladybug, part dragonfly talked so fast it was hard to tell anything he said.

Nathan raced to the switch on the wall and turned off the fan. Aristophenix didn't wait for it to stop:

Thank ya, dear Nathan,
there ain't a second to waste.
The Weaver, he's a callin',
so we better make haste.

Joshua and Nathan exchanged glances. The Weaver—the one assigned by the Imager to weave their life's tapestries, the kind old man who had helped save both of their lives—was calling *them* to Fayrah!

"But . . . what about Denise?" Joshua asked. "Doesn't he want her to come, too?"

Denny's the reason
we're under such stress.
She's dreamin' up somethin'
that's gonna cause quite a mess.

Again Joshua and Nathan traded looks.

"But, we can't just leave," Nathan explained. "Grandpa's not back from his deliveries. There's nobody to look after the—"

"About the store don't worry," Listro Q interrupted. "This part of world, freeze in time we will."

It didn't take Joshua long to piece together Listro Q's backward speaking. "You mean you're going to freeze time again, make it stand still?" he asked.

"But only here at store. Rest of world, normal time it will be."

As the most scientifically minded of the group, Josh had a couple thousand questions to ask about the procedure, but Samson barged in with a quick chatter.

Aristophenix nodded, "Good thinkin', Sammy."

"What's he saying?" Nathan asked.

Listro Q translated. "Mr. Hornsberry, here, is he?"

"My stuffed bulldog? Well, no, he's at home."

"Then swing by your home, better we do."

"Why?"

Aristophenix explained:

This adventure's gonna be tricky,
but his help we can not skip.
I know he's a snob, and a pain,
but we must overlook his snooty lip.

It's true. Nathan's stuffed bulldog *was* a snob. And he *was* snooty. But it sounded as if they were going to need all the man, and, er, dog power they could get.

"Canteen of Imager's water," Listro Q asked, "still do you have?"

"Not anymore," Josh replied. "We used it all up in the Sea of Mirrors."

"Then loan you my own," Listro Q said as he removed the large waterskin from his neck.

Joshua took it and quickly slipped it around his shoulders.

"Ready to go we are, if you are." Listro Q held the Cross-Dimensionalizer in his hand.

The brothers nodded. Without a word Listro Q punched in the four quadrants:

> Beep . . .
>> Bop . . .
>>> Burp . . .
>>>> Bleep . . .

and they were off.

—CHAPTER TWO—

DREAM ON

Denise woke with a start. For a minute she didn't know where she was—until she felt the jab of a steel armrest in her ribs, the sticky vinyl against her arms, and the cramp in her neck.

Ah, yes, the hospital chair.

She looked over at her mom, who was still asleep— the sedative was still working. In fact, in the dim morning light her mother looked peaceful, almost happy. It was a look Denny hadn't seen for years. Not really. Not real happiness. Not from her mom.

"Life is hard, then you die." That's what her mom always said. Of course, it was supposed to be funny, but Denise knew better. All she had to do was look around the hospital room and see it was no joke. Life was hard. Too hard.

Once again she felt the anger stirring inside. Anger

at what had happened. Anger at life. Anger at Imager's ways. If he was supposed to be so loving, then why were things always so hard? Why was there so much pain? Why was there any suffering at all?

Stewing in her anger, Denny remembered the dream. Not the dream about the ladder, but another dream. The one that was so strange yet so real. The one the Merchant of Emotions had planted.

In it she was upstairs in her uncle's attic . . . all alone. The large black trunk rested in front of her. Slowly, she knelt down to it. This is where she'd found the Bloodstone. This is where she and Nate had found Bud's cassette. And this is where the two of them had discovered the flat, thin stone at the very bottom.

Carefully, she lifted the trunk's heavy lid. It groaned in protest. On the top were clothes. Lots and lots of clothes. She began digging through them, deeper and deeper until she was at the bottom, until she finally felt it—the cold, smooth stone. She hauled it to the surface and set it on top. It was exactly as she remembered—a big flat rock—super thin, super smooth. Nothing more, nothing less.

Then the dream shifted slightly. Now she noticed faint blue lines running across the stone—lines like on notebook paper—lines that made it look like . . . well, like a writing tablet.

Next, a felt pen suddenly appeared in her hand. And then it was over—just like that. The dream ended and she woke up.

"Weird," Denise sighed. She glanced over to her mom, and then turned in her chair to go back to sleep.

But sleep wouldn't come. Not anymore. There was something too real about that dream, something too real about that stone. She lay in the chair wide awake, staring into the dark. Wondering. No matter how hard she tried, all she could think about was the stone and those faint little blue lines.

She didn't know how long she had lain there. Maybe an hour, maybe two. But she finally had enough. Throwing off the blanket, she looked at her watch.

6:50.

She hated to cross town and wake up her aunt this early. She knew the lady would think she was strange. Then again, Denny's whole family thought she was strange, so what was one more person added to the list?

Denise turned back to her mom. She was still sedated, still sleeping. "I'll be back in a few minutes," Denny whispered. "I just gotta check something out."

She pulled herself from the chair, grabbed her jacket, and headed for the door.

———

By now Joshua and Nathan were pretty used to traveling across dimensions. They were used to the blinding light and the sensation of falling. They were even used to seeing themselves as Imager saw them— Joshua as some sort of water bearer in a burlap robe and Nathan as a knight in glowing armor. There was one addition, though. Nathan was now carrying a large, rectangular shield.

This is great, Nathan thought to the others. (Speaking wasn't necessary when cross-dimensionalizing.) *I suppose I have to lug this shield thing along with me, now.*

The others looked on sympathetically. The shield was pretty good sized and it did look heavy.

Well, at least you won't have your limp, Josh thought back, trying to encourage him.

It was true. Whenever they appeared as Imager saw them, Nathan's painful limp completely disappeared.

Master Nathan, Master Nathan . . .

They turned to see Mr. Hornsberry, Nathan's stuffed bulldog, traveling beside them.

How fortunate it must be for you all to see me again.

Moments earlier they had dropped by Nathan's room to pick him up. Back there he was just as dead and lifeless as any other stuffed dog. But here he was alive and back to his usual snooty self.

How you doing, Mr. Hornsberry? Nathan thought.

As well as might be expected, having been confined to your closet these many months.

Sorry about—

I trust you're aware of the distinct aroma those gym socks in the corner have been emitting.

Before Nathan could answer, Aristophenix jumped in:

Good to see ya, ol' boy,
but we're a comin' to the Center.
Best be thinkin' them good thoughts,
so more gently you'll enter.

The dog glanced down and saw that they were approaching the brightly lit city. *Absolutely,* he thought, *quite right.*

Like the others, he closed his eyes and began thinking of Imager's greatness. Some of the group started to sing, others hummed, others simply smiled. But no matter what they did, their purpose was the same—to dwell on Imager's greatness, to join with the rest of the Universe in their love and adoration of him.

Soon they passed through a thin layer of clouds, and moments later they landed in the Center.

Nathan and Joshua looked about in awe. Although they'd been to the Center several times, their reaction was always the same. Amazement. Amazement and wonder. They were amazed at the beautiful lights. They marveled at the wonderous colors—amazing lights and wonderous colors that were actually creatures. Yet the creatures were only reflections of Imager's greater light and color. A light and color that blazed brilliantly just over the nearby ridge.

Then there was the music. It came from everywhere—the trees, the grass, even their own bodies. Everything vibrated with incredible chords and beautiful melodies—all directed toward Imager.

But this time something was different. "Nathan!" Josh cried. "Look at us! We're not shadows anymore. We're real!"

Nathan looked at Josh, then down at himself. It was true. In their past visits to the Center they had barely been visible. They had been like faint shadows. It's not that they weren't real, it's just that everything around them had been so much *more* real. But now, all of that had changed.

Nathan tapped his armor. "You can't see through me!" he cried. "I'm totally here! We're both totally here!"

Samson buzzed their heads and chattered an explanation. Aristophenix translated:

It's cause you're re-Breathed,
now you got Imager's presence.
You're no longer just shadows,
since you're filled with his essence.

" 'Cause he's inside us?" Josh asked. "That's what makes us real?"

Listro Q nodded. "Ever since Whirlwind filled you, as real now you are as . . ." He turned toward the light glowing behind the ridge. "As real now you are as Imager."

The group turned in awe toward the hill, toward the light blazing behind it. A light so brilliant it made all the others dim by comparison. But it was more than just light. It had a quality, a type of "splendor" about it. A splendor so intense that it nearly destroyed Denise on an earlier trip.

As they gazed upon the light, a question slowly formed in Joshua's mind. "Aristophenix? Aristophenix could we, you know, maybe see him? Now that we're solid and real and everything . . . would it be safe to see Imager?"

"Are you crazy?!" Nathan cried. Nathan knew Josh loved to take risks. In fact, Joshua had more confidence in his little finger than Nate had in his entire body. Most of the time that made Nathan jealous. Other times, like now, it scared him to death. "You know what happened when Denny tried to see him!"

"But it's different now," Joshua insisted. "We're re-Breathed." He turned to Listro Q and Aristophenix. "Right, fellas?"

The Fayrahnians exchanged uneasy looks. According to their calculations, Denny was already awake from her dream and was heading for her uncle's attic. They had little time to spare. Yet, how could they, mere Fayrahnians, say no to an Upside-Downer's request to see Imager?

Samson chattered something, and with a heavy sigh Aristophenix finally agreed:

Well, if that's what you want,
I ain't gonna spoil it.
But we gotta hurry and save
yer world from, uh . . . the toilet!

The group groaned as they started toward the ridge. Somehow they had hoped his poetry would improve in a place like this. Wrong again.

———

Denise heaved open the lid to the trunk. It gave a heavy groan—just like in her dream. She peered inside and began digging through the clothes—just like in the dream.

Her aunt, a frail lady, stood at the top of the attic stairs clutching her robe against the early morning chill. She watched silently as Denise plowed through the old clothes and oddities.

"What's this?" Denny asked as she pulled out something she thought looked like a camera. But this camera had no lens. In fact, it was impossible to tell the front from the back. Or the top from the bottom.

"You know your uncle," the woman sighed. "Just something he brought back from one of his trips. We'll have to ask him when he returns."

Denise looked at her. The woman smiled weakly. Her husband had been gone nearly two years. At first he'd started returning from his filming expeditions with strange and weird tales about strange and weird places. Then one day he disappeared and never returned at all. Everyone knew he wasn't coming back—everyone but his wife. Well, maybe she knew, too. Maybe she just wanted to keep hoping.

At last Denny reached the bottom of the trunk. She

felt the smooth flat stone lying there and carefully pulled it out.

It was the same as in the dream.

Well, almost the same. The only difference was there were no lines on the rock. Try as she might, Denny could not find the notebook lines she had seen in her dream. Nor was there any felt pen.

Denny scowled.

"What's wrong, honey?" her aunt asked.

"Something's not right."

Without a word she plowed through the trunk again.

Nothing.

She plopped down on the floor cross-legged. Pulling the Tablet onto her lap, she began drumming her fingers on it, trying to think. The surface was smooth and hard, but not so hard that she couldn't make faint marks with her fingernails.

Finally her aunt turned and started for the steps. "I'll be downstairs if you need me."

"Thanks, Aunt Margaret."

The woman headed down the steps as Denny continued to ponder. Oh sure, she knew it had only been a dream. But everything seemed so real, as if it were really going to happen. So why weren't there any lines on the Tablet? Why no pen to write with? As she sat there thinking it over, Denny absentmindedly scratched her name onto the soft stone with her fingernail.

D-E-N . . .

It was no big deal, just faint markings she could wipe off anytime.

. . . I-S . . .

Then, when she carved the final "E," it happened. . . .

Suddenly she felt the presence of another person in the room! She spun around and caught her breath. Not because she was frightened. There was nothing to be frightened about. This was not some strange creature from some strange dimension. This was no alien monster. In fact, Denny knew this person. She knew this person very well. For there, directly in front of Denise Wolff stood . . . Denise Wolff!

Somehow, by writing her name on the Tablet, Denny had created another Denny, one exactly like herself!

CHAPTER THREE

A LITTLE STOPOVER

Even with his clumsy suit of armor and the heavy shield, Nathan was only a few steps behind Josh as they raced for the top of the knoll. He wasn't crazy about the idea of seeing Imager, but he was even less crazy about being left behind.

Suddenly there was a blinding flash of light just on the other side.

"What's that?" Josh cried.

Aristophenix was pulling up the rear by a dozen yards. His pudgy little body couldn't keep pace with the others, but between wheezes he managed to gasp:

Must be graduation (*pant, puff*)
for Upside-Downers, take a peek.
Go see what's in store (*wheeze, gasp*)
when your lives are complete.

Joshua and Nathan reached the top of the ridge

just in time to be hit by another flash of light. It was so bright, so intense, that it knocked both of them to the ground. Now it's hard to believe that light can knock a person to the ground, but when you find yourself lying face first in the dirt, well, it's a little easier to imagine. You see, this was more than just light. It was a type of power, a type of . . . presence—so pure, so powerful, that it carried quite a wallop.

Now Joshua and Nathan were no fools. Since they were already on the ground, and since they were scared to death, they figured it wouldn't hurt to lie there just a little longer. You see, they kind of enjoyed living life and they just weren't sure how long that would continue living if they got up. So there they stayed, covering their heads—Nathan with his shield, Joshua with his arms.

But Josh couldn't stay that way forever. No sir. After all, wasn't he one of the most popular guys in school? Hadn't his team won the district basketball championship? Wasn't he nearly elected Student Body President? What did he have to fear?

Actually a lot! Somehow he suspected basketball trophies and student elections wouldn't come in all that handy at the moment. But you couldn't stop his curiosity. Call it scientific investigation or just plain stupidity, it didn't matter. The point is, Josh *had* to see. He *had* to know. So with eyes clinched tight, he leaned over and whispered to his brother, "Now what?"

"What do you mean, 'now what'?" Nathan's voice echoed in fear under the shield.

"I mean, we can't just stay on our faces like this."

"Oh, I bet we can," Nathan offered. "I got a few more things I want to do before croaking."

"Imager's not going to kill us."

"How do you know?"

"Listro Q says he's too cool, too loving. C'mon. Don't you want to take just a little peek to see for yourself?"

"I'll take their word for it. Now just lie down and keep still."

"Aristophenix—?"

"Josh, will you keep—"

Again Joshua called, "Aristophenix . . . Listro Q?"

There was no answer. Only another flash. A flash so bright that even with their eyes closed and heads covered they could feel its power wash over them.

That was it. Josh could stand no more. Live or die (although the living part still sounded a lot better), he had to see. Slowly, ever so slowly, he lifted one arm from his head.

So far so good.

Then the other arm.

No heart attack yet. No instant vaporization. Good signs.

He opened one eye, just enough to take a quick peek—just enough to see Aristophenix, Listro Q, Samson, even Mr. Hornsberry, all on their knees, their faces bowed to the ground in the direction of the light.

Slowly, he turned his head in the direction of the light. It grew brighter and brighter but he kept turning. The back of his eyes started to ache, but he pressed on. He had to. Finally, he was looking directly into the center of the light. And there he saw . . .

Nothing.

Well, at first nothing. It was too bright to see anything. But as he squinted his eyes he slowly made out a large, broad plain that stretched below them. It was so clear and so smooth that it almost looked like water. But it couldn't be water. There were too many creatures standing on it. Millions of glowing creatures.

And they were singing. They were all singing to an even brighter figure standing in the center of the plain—a Figure carved out of the most intense, blazing light imaginable. Light brighter than the sun. Brighter than a thousand suns.

Josh squinted harder. You didn't have to be a genius to figure out who that Figure was. At first it stood directly in the middle of the plain. Then, suddenly, it was standing much closer. Then far off in the distance. Then somewhere to Josh's left. Then to his right. It was pretty confusing. As if it were everywhere at the same time.

Then there was its face. . . .

Actually, it was too bright to see the face, but there was no missing the profile—a profile that kept changing. One minute it was a giant bird, like an eagle; the next, some sort of bull; then an innocent lamb, followed by a lion . . . On and on it went. Changing again and again and again.

It was too much. Josh's mind began to spin. Everything was too strange, too weird. He was growing dizzy. His brain started to fry, to overload. Then suddenly he heard a voice. It shook the ground like thunder. It was so loud it made his ears ring . . . and yet, at the same time it was soft and tender.

"HELLO, JOSHUA."

Josh spun around and gasped. The Figure was kneeling directly beside him! His mind reeled. Still, he had to see. He had to look into the face. Slowly he looked up. When their gaze finally met, he saw the eyes were as powerful as the voice . . . *and* as tender. They blazed with a type of fire—a fire that burned into Joshua's mind.

But the boy couldn't look away.

The eyes began searching his thoughts—seeing his deepest, darkest secrets. Things no one knew. Things he did in secret, said in secret, thought in secret. Things that embarrassed him beyond belief. Suddenly they were all exposed, all lit up. Suddenly every thought and action of Joshua O'Brien was in plain view of those eyes.

But Josh felt no fear. Because as penetrating as those eyes were, as much as they revealed his darkest secrets, they didn't condemn those secrets. If anything, they seemed to love and understand Josh more *because* of those secrets.

It took Joshua forever to find his voice. Finally he was able to squeak out a little, "Who . . ." But that was as far as he got. He was too overcome to speak.

The figure understood perfectly. He motioned toward the plain below them, toward all the different appearances of himself.

"*I* AM *HE*."

Josh wasn't sure if he was going to lose his mind or just curl up and die on the spot. But for some reason he did neither. It probably had something to do with those marvelous eyes.

He tried to ask another question. "How . . ." But he shook his head. He had no business asking anything. He had no business saying anything. In fact, at that moment he had no business *being* anything.

The eyes looked on kindly. The voice roared and whispered,

"ASK YOUR QUESTION, JOSHUA O'BRIEN."

Josh swallowed hard. "How . . . how can you be here . . . and down there at the same time? You're everywhere at once."

"YES, *I* AM."

"But . . . one minute you're a bird, then an animal, then—"

"YOUR MIND CANNOT GRASP *MY* FULLNESS, SO IT SEES *ME* IN SYMBOLS."

"But—"

"LOOK. . . ."

The Figure pointed to a withered old woman on the plain below them. Unlike the others, she was shriveled and crippled. And unlike the others, she was *not* glowing.

He continued. His voice lowered in quiet reverence:

"SHE'S AN UPSIDE-DOWNER . . . LIKE YOU."

"You mean she's cross-dimensionalized just like—"

"NO. SHE HAS GRADUATED."

"Graduated?"

"WATCH."

Joshua looked back to the plain. The glowing Figure of Light was now standing beside the woman. Josh looked back to his own side. The Figure of Light was also there. "OK," the boy sighed, trying to get a grip. "I can handle this. I hope . . ."

He turned back to the plain and watched as the old woman crumpled to the Figure's feet and began sobbing. But she wasn't the only one crying. So was the Figure.

A hush fell over the plain. All singing came to a stop. The millions of creatures watched in speechless anticipation as the Figure slowly stooped down to join the old woman. At last he spoke:

"*I* HAVE BEEN WAITING A LONG TIME FOR YOU."

The woman looked up. Tears streamed down her face. Tears streamed down both of their faces. Slowly, the Figure reached out his hands and helped her as the two rose to their feet. Then, even more tenderly, he began to wipe the tears from her cheeks. She looked into his eyes, her face glowing with love and adoration. Finally, he drew her into a deep, heartfelt embrace.

And with that embrace the most amazing thing happened. . . .

There was another flash of light. Josh ducked his head as the wave of power roared over him. It lasted several seconds. When it was finally safe to look up, he saw that the woman was still in the Figure's arms. But she was different now . . . much different. Now, she glowed. Now she shared a part of the Figure's brilliance—a part of his power. No longer was she bent and crippled. Now she was beautiful. Radiant. Now she was young, powerful and glowing with the Figure's own glory.

The two continued gazing into each other's eyes . . . like lovers brought together after years of separation. Finally the Figure took her hand in his. He said only four words.

"COME . . . SIT WITH *ME*."

The entire plain broke into applause . . . then shouts and cheers as the couple turned and headed through the throng.

Josh looked on. His eyes burned with tears. The back of his throat ached with emotion. He turned to the Figure of Light which was now beside him. He tried to speak but it came out thick and raspy. "Do you . . . do that with everyone?"

There was no missing the moisture in the Figure's own eyes as he smiled.

"*I* DO THAT WITH *MY* FRIENDS."

———

Back in the attic Denise stared at the newly created Denise. But never known for her shyness, the first Denise immediately demanded, "Who are you?"

"I'm you," the new Denise answered.

"You mean you're a picture of me—like a holograph."

"No, I'm you."

"But . . . how . . ."

"How should I know? You're the one who wrote me."

"Wrote. . . ?"

"Didn't you just write my name on the Tablet?"

Denise looked at the flat stone on her lap. "Well, no—how could I? I don't have anything to write—"

"With your fingernail," the new Denise sighed. "You scratched my name on the Tablet with your fingernail."

"So?"

"So here I am."

"You mean . . . whatever I write on this thing—"

"—happens, yeah."

"Let me get this straight. You're saying that whatever I write on this *Tablet* becomes real?"

The new Denise shook her head and muttered, "I didn't know I was so stupid. Yes! Yes!" she shouted at the old Denise. "Whatever you write on that Tablet becomes—"

But she never finished . . . for immediately Denise reached over and rubbed off the name and the second Denise disappeared.

She rose unsteadily to her feet. Was this really happening? Could this thing . . . this "Tablet" . . . really create anything she wanted? Balancing the stone on one hand, she started to scratch in another word until she noticed her fingernail was wearing thin. She changed her mind and wrote F-E-L-T P-E-N instead.

Instantly there was a black felt pen in her hand.

Denny's mind raced with possibilities. What were the limits? *Were* there any limits? She started to scrawl out C-A-R, then quickly changed it to L-I-M-O-U-S-I-N-E (all the time hoping she was spelling it right).

She raced to the window and looked out. Sure enough—there, parked outside the house, was a black, shiny limo.

Denny leaned against the wall for support. This was too incredible. With the Tablet she could make anything she wanted. But *things* had never interested her much (well, except for a limo or two). One look at her wardrobe told you that material stuff wasn't that big a deal to her.

Then why, she wondered, was she the one given the

. . . wait a minute. Of course! That was it! That's why she had the dream! That's why she found the Tablet! She wasn't led to it to fulfill her own selfish desires. She was led to the Tablet to make the world a better place!

The thought caused Denny to shudder, to breathe faster. What an honor! What a privilege! But it made sense. She, Denise Wolff, had been chosen to change the world! Think of it! She could actually make it better. She could do away with suffering, with poverty, with injustice. She could make everything—PER-FECT!

This was no "genie in a lamp" time. No "make three wishes and get whatever you want." Forget the things, forget the big screen TVs, the fame, the fortune. Denise was chosen for something greater. She was chosen to change the world—to do away with wars, hunger, disease. What a calling! What a challenge! But she was certain she could meet it.

She felt the weight of the Tablet in her hand—its power, its possibilities. But where to begin? The world was in such a mess; where should she start?

How about something small? she thought. *Yeah, that's it. For starters, I should begin with something—*

She had it! If she wanted to end all pain and suffering, how about starting off with her mom? Her mom who was filled with so much pain at the hospital!

She raised the Tablet and wrote:

N-O   P-A-I-N.

There. Finished. She waited in anticipation. But nothing happened. Everything was the same. She glanced back out the window. The limo was still there, but nothing else had changed. Or had it? There was only one way to find out. She turned and raced down the stairs.

Joshua didn't know how long their conversation lasted. It could have been hours, it could have been minutes, it could have been seconds. But by the way Nathan, Aristophenix, and the gang were still frozen on their knees, he voted for seconds.

The blazing Figure of Light continued talking. His voice as powerful and tender as ever:

"*MY* BELOVED UPSIDE-DOWN KINGDOM IS IN DANGER."

"Yes," Josh answered, "I know, but how—"

"DEAR DENISE . . ."

For a moment Joshua thought he heard a sigh.

"SHE NO LONGER TRUSTS *ME*.
SHE IS CREATING A DIFFERENT WORLD.
A WORLD SHE THINKS IS BETTER THAN *MINE*.
A WORLD TO WHICH SHE WILL INVITE
THE MERCHANT OF EMOTIONS."

"Merchant of Emotions?"

"HE CONTROLS THROUGH EMOTIONS."

"But how . . . what can we do?"
The Figure smiled warmly at Josh's concern.

"YOU WILL DEFEAT HIM.
AS *MY* WATER BEARER, YOU HAVE *MY* WORD.
AS *MY* ARMOR BEARER, NATHAN HAS *MY* FAITH.
TOGETHER YOU WILL HELP DENNY UNDER-
STAND."

"Yes, but why won't—"

"WHY WON'T *I* STOP HER?"

Joshua nodded.

"DENNY NO LONGER LISTENS TO *ME*."

"You could make her."

A brief look of pain crossed those magnificent eyes.

"SHE MUST TRUST *ME* BECAUSE SHE WANTS TO,
NOT BECAUSE *I* MAKE HER.
COME."

He gently helped Joshua to his feet.

Of course, Josh wanted to say more . . .

. . . like, the only thing he and his brother ever succeeded at together was fighting, so how could they save the world?

. . . like, why couldn't Imager just do it?

. . . like, why did he need their help?

But Josh didn't say a word. Imager already knew. He reached out and set a powerful hand on the boy's shoulder.

"YOU ARE *MY* FEET, JOSHUA O'BRIEN.
YOU ARE *MY* HANDS.
YOU ARE *MY* VOICE."

Never in his life had Joshua felt so proud . . . or so helpless.

Sensing the boy's fear, the Figure drew him into an embrace. There was no flash of light. No transfer of energy. No graduation. Only the warmth and love of Imager holding his beloved. Joshua wanted to stay buried there forever, but he knew he couldn't. At least not now.

Finally they separated. Josh brushed the tears from his eyes and looked up just in time to catch the

Figure touching his own eyes. "Will I . . . ever see you again?" the boy asked.

The Figure broke into a grin.

**"YES, *MY* FRIEND, YOU WILL SEE *ME*.
YOU WILL SEE *ME* WHENEVER YOU LOOK."**

With that Joshua suddenly found himself standing in Fayrah. No cross-dimensionalizing, no traveling—one minute he was standing before Imager; the next, he and the entire group were standing in one of Fayrah's Great Halls of Tapestry.

— CHAPTER FOUR —

CHANGES

The Halls of Tapestry were as dazzling as ever. In each of the giant rooms hung thousands of tapestries. Beautiful, shimmering tapestries woven from glowing threads of light. Each was a masterpiece. Each represented a life Imager had imaged. Every living creature ever created had his, her, or its own tapestry hanging in one of these magnificent halls.

Joshua was the first to spot the Weaver. The old man was at the far end of the room, pacing back and forth between tapestries. Even at that distance Josh could tell he was concerned.

As the group approached, the Weaver glanced up. "You're late" was all he said before turning back to the tapestries.

Aristophenix tried to explain:

They wanted to see Imager,
a request we can not shrug.
And by the glow on ol' Josh's face,
it was somethin' he dug.

The Weaver shuddered. He'd never understood why Imager had asked him to weave that awful thread of poetry into Aristophenix's life. But there it was, just as dreadful to listen to as ever.

"What's the problem?" Nathan asked as he clinked a step or two closer in his armor. "And why are we still wearing these stupid outfits?"

"Those are your offices," the Weaver explained. "Yes they are."

"But it's three sizes too big," Nathan whined as he tried to adjust the armor. "And this shield thing weighs a ton." Now Nathan didn't mean to whine. That was just his nature. As sure as Denise had her temper and Josh his ego, Nathan had his whine.

"You will grow into that armor," the Weaver patiently explained. "And the shield will come in most handy."

"Yes, but—"

"This is how he has imaged you, yes it is. And this is how you will stop the Merchant."

"The Merchant?" Nathan repeated.

It was Josh's turn to explain. "The Merchant of Emotions. Imager said that—"

"Wait a minute, you talked to Imager? When?"

"I'll explain later. The point is—"

"I want to know now, when did you talk to—"

"Nathan, for once in your life try not to be the world's biggest brat."

"Who're you calling a—"

"Gentlemen, gentlemen," the Weaver sighed. "I know it's difficult to be civil to each other, but if you will look at these tapestries, you'll see we have little time."

The boys turned back to the tapestries in front of them. Something was wrong. They could see it at once. The intricate beauty of their patterns was disappearing.

Listro Q was the first to speak. "Tapestries coming unraveled their weave."

It was true, each of the tapestries was slowly unraveling. Dozens of beautiful designs were coming undone. The glowing threads were pulling out of their weave and hanging haphazardly in all directions.

"What's happening?" Josh cried. "They're coming apart!"

"An inappropriate observation." It was Mr. Hornsberry. "Upon closer examination you will note many of the tapestries are actually reweaving themselves."

The group stepped closer for a better look. It was true. Some of the threads were actually coming together again, intertwining, forming their own patterns. But instead of the beautiful, glowing masterpieces, they were forming gross, clumsy designs.

Samson chattered off a quick question.

The Weaver shook his head and answered, "No, only the tapestries from the Upside-down Kingdom are being rewoven."

"But why. . . ?" Nathan stammered. "Who's responsible?"

The Weaver turned directly to the boy. He said only one word . . .

"Denise."

The group stood dumbfounded.

"But how. . . ?" Josh asked. "How could Denise, how could one person do all this damage?"

The Weaver turned and started toward one of the tapestries. He pushed it aside to reveal a huge door. "Come."

The group glanced at one another, then obeyed.

"Where are we going?" Nathan asked.

The Weaver saw no need to answer, so Aristophenix did the honors:

If I ain't too mistaken,
you'll enjoy this little stroll.
Normally Upside-Downers are forbidden
to enter someone's Master Control.

The Weaver heaved open the door and entered. The others followed.

———

Denise couldn't believe what she saw as her limo turned in to the hospital parking lot. Outside there were hundreds of people. Most were wearing those silly little hospital gowns—the type that never quite close in the back. But no one seemed to care. Not anymore. Everyone was too excited.

The limo stopped and Denny threw open the door. It was chaos. Everywhere patients were running and leaping and laughing.

"What's going on?" she shouted as she stepped into the mob. "What's happening?"

No one heard.

"Would somebody please tell me what's happening?"

Finally an old man turned to her. He was very frail and very, very pale. But he was grinning. From ear to ear his toothless gums glistened in the sunlight. "Haven't you heard? We're healed! There ain't no pain no more!" With that he leaped into the air to kick his heels. Of course, he failed miserably and fell to the ground in a crumpled heap. But he didn't care, not in the least—unless you call breaking into uncontrollable laughter "caring."

Denny looked around in disbelief. The place was like a carnival. Old-timers laughed and ran like children. Pregnant mothers jumped rope and played tag. Cancer patients slapped one another on the back, hooting and hollering with joy.

The only ones not smiling were the doctors. "Please, you are not well!" they kept shouting. "You must come back to your rooms."

But no one listened. Why should they? The doctors were obviously wrong. There was no pain. No one was suffering. Not anymore.

And Denny knew why. She couldn't help grinning down at the Tablet in her hands. *N-O   P-A-I-N* was still written on the stone. *She* had done this. *She, Denise Wolff,* had single-handedly rid the world of pain. With just two words she had erased all of the world's misery and suffering. Her chest swelled with pride. She shook her head in wonder. She was good. She was very, very good.

She started through the crowd to look for her mom. After all, her mother was the inspiration for all this. "Mom . . . Mom, where are you?"

"Clear the way!" A couple of wheelchair patients raced by. "Clear the way!" They nearly knocked Denise to the ground as they sped past. "Sorry!" they shouted as they disappeared into the crowd.

"Don't worry," Denny called back. "You couldn't hurt me if you tried!"

She wasn't bragging, just stating a fact. They

couldn't hurt her. They couldn't hurt *anyone*. She had made the world too good for that. She wasn't sure why Imager had created the mess he had, but she was sure of one thing . . . with the Tablet she was going to clean it up. She was going to make it better, *a lot* better. She drew the stone closer and searched the crowd. "Mom . . . Mom . . ."

"Denny! Denny, over here!"

Denise turned and spotted her mother hobbling through the crowd. Her face was glowing. All trace of suffering was gone. Instead, she was doing her best to ignore a worried nurse who was pleading for her to sit down.

"Please, Mrs. Wolff, your leg's not ready—"

"Don't be silly. I'm fine, just fine."

Denise's grin widened as she pushed through the crowd toward her mother. She couldn't wait to tell her mom the secret that she alone was responsible for—

Then her mom came into view and Denny's joy turned to horror.

"Mother, your leg!"

The woman glanced down at her hospital gown. The lower portion was spattered with blood. But it wasn't the blood that frightened Denny. It was the way the leg was all turned and twisted in different directions again.

"I told her it wasn't healed," the nurse cried. "I told her it wouldn't hold her—"

"Nonsense," Mrs. Wolff laughed. "I feel fine. It doesn't bother me a—"

*   "But, Mom . . . it looks awful. And what's this white

*This section may be too intense for reading to younger children. Please see the preface in *The Portal*.

• 49 •

thing?" Denise bent down for a better look. She wished she hadn't. The "white thing" was the leg bone! It was still broken, still twisted, and now it was jutting through her skin!

"Mom, sit down!"

"Sweetheart, I—"

"SIT DOWN!"

Reluctantly the woman let Denny help her to the ground.

"IS THERE A DOCTOR?!" Denny shouted to the crowd. "PLEASE, I NEED A DOCTOR! I NEED A DOCTOR RIGHT NOW!"

— Chapter Five —

The Chase
Begins

"Wow!" both boys exclaimed as they entered the large circular room. Running around the outside perimeter, like a giant ring, was a desk top. And sitting at the desk, facing toward the center, were nearly two dozen Fayrahnians. Each carefully studied a little 3-D picture that floated before them. Each carefully adjusted the complex knobs and controls on the desk below the pictures. But that was nothing compared to what floated in the center of the room.

For there, directly in the center, nearly twenty feet high, was a giant 3-D projection of Denise! She was in a hospital room arguing with two doctors and a nurse over her mother's broken and bleeding leg.

The Weaver explained to the brothers as quickly as possible. "Behind each tapestry is a door leading to that person's Master Control."

"You mean each of us has a room like this?" Josh asked.

"Of course."

The boys exchanged looks.

"My assistants here carefully monitor the decisions you make in your weave."

"Hold it," Nathan interrupted. "I thought you wove those tapestries the way Imager told you."

"I do."

"Then how—"

"You still have free will. If you refuse Imager's design, you may change it."

"But," Josh argued, "who would want to? I mean, his designs are so incredible."

The Weaver nodded and sighed heavily. "Yours is a most stubborn king, Joshua O'Brien. Many insist on their own weave instead of Imager's." He motioned to the circular desk and continued. "Here we monitor your every decision, yes we do. Down to the tiniest details."

"The details?"

"They are often what change your life the most."

Josh looked at him skeptically.

"Not at first, but five, ten, twenty years in the future. It is the little choices that change your life. The tiny choices are often—" He was interrupted by a loud, buzzing alarm.

"Sir!" a nearby assistant cried, "we have another Code 12!"

The Weaver quickly crossed to the assistant's station to study the little 3-D picture floating before him. It was another image of Denise, but in a much different location. "Put it on the big screen!"

The assistant obeyed. Immediately the big-screen

image of Denise in the hospital was replaced by another one. In it she looked awful. She was haggard and very, very frightened. Instead of her usual uniform of baggy pants and T-shirt she wore some sort of fancy riding habit. And she carried a large flat stone.

She was standing on a beach next to a burning bus. Headed in her direction was a mob of people—some crawling, others staggering. But they all had one thing in common. Their hatred for Denise."YOU'RE THE REASON!" they screamed as they rushed at her. "IT'S YOUR FAULT! YOU STOPPED THE SHOW!"

Denise stumbled backward.

The mob continued forward. "BORING!" they screamed. "YOU ARE BORING!"

"It's not true!" Denise cried. "I've made things better!"

* Suddenly she heard other voices. "The Tablet! Get the Tablet!!" She spun around to see another group. Thousands of them. They were awful to look at. Their bodies were broken and twisted beyond belief. Like the others, they crawled and staggered toward her. "Get the Tablet, get the Tablet, get the Tablet . . ."

The nightmare closed in from every side. "YOUR FAULT!" others shrieked. "YOU ARE EVIL—*EVIL!*"

"Please!" Denise screamed. But it did no good. "Mr. Hornsberry, Samson—do something!"

Back in Master Control the picture on the screen widened. It was a shock for Mr. Hornsberry and Samson to see themselves up on the screen, but neither spoke a word.

"Don't you understand?!" Denise pleaded as the mob closed in on her. "I've made things better!"

"You've made our lives boring!" a drug-crazed girl screamed.

"Unspeakable!" a horribly burnt man cried.

"Unlivable!" a twisted creature shrieked. "You must be stopped!"

They were nearly on top of her.

Back in Master Control, Josh turned to the Weaver and shouted, "This is what will happen in the future?"

The Weaver nodded. "*If* she makes the wrong decision in the hospital."

"What's that in her hand?" Nathan yelled, referring to the flat stone she carried.

Aristophenix explained:

The Tablet she has found,
it changes reality.
It's the thing that will bring
all of this calamity.

Joshua turned back to the Weaver for a further explanation.

"This is the future!" the Weaver shouted. "Yes it is. This is what will happen if Denise keeps changing Imager's reality."

"It's awful!" Nathan cried.

"It's nothing compared to what will follow." The Weaver turned to another assistant. "Punch up thirty seconds from this. Thirty seconds into the future after she's written on the Tablet."

The assistant obeyed. The pleading Denise disappeared from the screen and was replaced by another creature. It was large with claws, crystal clear scales, and huge black leathery wings. Wings that carried it silently through space toward a blue, cloud-covered planet that could only be—

"Earth!" Joshua cried. "He's heading for earth!"

The Weaver nodded sadly.

"That's the Illusionist!" Nathan shouted. "I thought she was dead. I thought we destroyed her."

"Closely, look more," Listro Q called. "The Illusionist it is not. Her brother it is."

"Her brother?"

The Weaver explained. "He's called the Merchant of Emotions, yes he is. He is the creature you must battle, the one you must stop from entering the Upside-down Kingdom."

"But he's almost there. How can we stop—"

"Remember, this is the future you're seeing."

"Yeah, but—"

"Punch up II–17 Quadrant E," the Weaver ordered.

An assistant transferred another image to the center screen. It was a kingdom of towering buildings, crowded roadways, and deafening noise. Noise like a thousand stereos blasting at once.

"This is where he has landed for now. He has already enslaved this kingdom as he waits to attack yours. This is where you must stop him."

"But, how?" Joshua demanded. "Imager said something about Nathan's suit of armor and I'm supposed to—"

The Weaver nodded. "Nathan believes in Imager more strongly than you. That armor and shield are his belief, his protection from the Merchant's powers."

"What about me?"

"You are the water bearer. You have Imager's water in that waterskin."

Josh instinctively adjusted the waterskin around his shoulder that Listro Q had given him.

"Imager's liquid words and letters are your weapon."

"What good is—"

"Remember how the water melted Seerlo?"

"Well, yes, but—"

"How it helped you see as Imager sees."

"Sure, but—"

"Its power will surprise you, yes it will."

"Hold it," Nathan interrupted. "You're telling us that—"

Suddenly another alarm sounded.

The Weaver spun to the screen. "There's no time to explain!" he shouted. "You must stop the Merchant of Emotions before he reaches your kingdom—before Denise invites him to your world." Turning to Listro Q, he called, "Have you entered their coordinates?"

"Yes, did I."

"Then give him one of your Cross-Dimensionalizers."

Listro Q reached over and handed Nathan the small control unit. "Still remember you, how to use it?"

"Well, yeah, but you guys are coming with me."

The Weaver shook his head. "Only the re-Breathed can handle Imager's weapons, only you will be able to stop the Merchant."

"But—"

"Go!"

"I still don't see how we can—"

It was Aristophenix's turn to be impatient:

Don't worry 'bout it,
we'll be here watchin' the show.
Just use them gifts wisely,
now hurry and go.

"Yes, but—"

Another alarm sounded.

"Go!" the Weaver ordered. "NOW!"

Joshua looked to his brother. Nathan took a deep breath, pressed the four buttons on the Cross-Dimensionalizer,

> Beep . . .
> > Bop . . .
> > > Burp . . .
> > > > Bleep . . .

and they were gone.

The Weaver took a deep breath of his own and looked to the rest of the group. "This one's going to be close," he sighed, "yes it is."

———

Back in the hospital, Denny kept clutching the Tablet and shaking her head at her mother's doctors—an older man and a younger one.

"You don't understand," the older doctor tried to reason. "Pain is good."

"No way!" Denise argued. "Pain causes suffering, it causes misery. Everything's better now that I got rid of it!"

"Are you blind?" The younger doctor was practically shouting. He pointed to her mom's twisted and bleeding leg. "You call that better?! Without pain she didn't know how bad she was injured. She kept walking on it, making it worse and worse!"

Denny didn't like the young doctor. Not one bit. He was rude and arrogant. "You're telling me," she scorned, "that we *need* pain?"

"Yes," the older doctor insisted. "It's nature's way of telling us something's wrong."

"You're crazy. I destroyed pain to make the world a better place!"

"You're wrong!" the younger doctor exploded.

"And you're jealous!" she shouted back. " 'Cause me and this Tablet just happened to put you out of business!"

"That's not it!" he yelled. "That's not it at all!" He stormed to the window. "LOOK!" Before anyone could stop him, he reached back and smashed his hand through the upper glass window.

The room gasped, "Doctor!"

He paid no attention. Instead, he held out his bleeding hand to her. "Look! No pain!" He spun around and smashed it through the lower window.

"DOCTOR!"

Again he held it out. Only now it was in worse shape than before. "Don't you see?" he pleaded. "I could do this all day and it wouldn't matter. I could get hit by a truck, burn myself, get sick—without pain I'd never know I needed help. Without pain I'd kill myself!"

But Denise's stubborn streak was at an all-time high. She had made the world a better place, and she wasn't about to let some doctor convince her to change it back. "No!" she insisted. "I made the change, and that's how it's going to stay!"

"We'll see about that," the younger doctor snapped as he suddenly lunged for the Tablet.

Denise screamed and jumped back.

"Get the Tablet!" he shouted.

The older doctor and accompanying nurse joined in. Seconds later the three had Denny pinned against the wall as they tried to yank the Tablet from her.

"Stop it!" Denny's mom yelled as she hobbled into the fight. "Stop it!"

Denise continued screaming but it did no good. Hands came at her from all sides. She dropped to the floor and wrapped herself around the Tablet. She began kicking and biting—anything to keep them at bay.

Then she saw it. Between their legs. An opening. And past that . . . the door. She scampered between the legs and leaped up. In an instant she was out the door and in the hall.

"Stop her! STOP HER!"

She sprinted down the hall and knocked a couple patients off their feet. But it didn't matter. Since they didn't feel pain, they just sat there laughing.

She came to the end of the hall, looked both directions, and darted to the right. She wasn't sure where she was going, but she could hear the younger doctor closing in from behind.

"Stop, Denise! Stop!"

No way.

An open doorway came into view. She dashed into the room and tried to shut the door and lock it. But the doctor was too fast. Before she could close it, he was pushing against it. She pushed back as hard as she could, but he continued to move it forward inch by inch. . . .

"Denise . . . be reasonable."

She was losing ground rapidly. Any second he would be inside. Suddenly she had an idea. If the Tablet could do anything, then maybe, just maybe . . . She pulled up the Tablet and fumbled for the felt pen.

"Denise . . ."

The door was nearly open. Already his arm and shoulder were squeezing in. Already he was reaching toward her.

Furiously, she scrawled out the letters until finally she had the words:

O-B-E-Y M-E!

But nothing happened! The doctor just kept coming! With a final push, he shoved through the opening and grabbed her! She screamed, but it did no good. Why?! What was wrong?!

"OK," he panted, "it's over. Give it to me." He held out his good hand, waiting.

Denny's mind raced. *Why didn't the Tablet work?*

"Denise . . ." He grabbed the Tablet, but she still wouldn't let go. "All right, if that's the way you want it. . . ." He started prying her fingers loose—one at a time.

Suddenly she had it. Of course! He hadn't obeyed because she hadn't given an order!

"Give it up, it's over. . . ." The Tablet was nearly in his hands. Just a couple more fingers to go. "Be a good girl now and let—"

"Stop it!" Denny commanded.

Immediately the doctor stopped. A look of confusion crossed his face. Finally he spoke. "I'm . . . I'm sorry, Ms. Wolff . . . I don't know what came over me."

Denny watched cautiously.

"I do hope you'll forgive me. May I walk you back to your mother's room?"

"Sure," Denise answered slowly as she pulled the Tablet in closer.

The doctor held the door open for her and they entered the corridor. Denny still wasn't a hundred percent sure. Was he just faking it or had the Tablet really worked? And if it worked, did that mean that no matter what she asked, he would have to obey her? Denise hated to do it, but there was really only one way to find out.

"Excuse me, Doctor?"

"Yes."

"Would you bark like a dog for me, please."

The man instantly dropped to his knees and began to bark and howl.

Everyone in the hallway stared in amazement. Everyone but Denise. "Thank you, Doctor," she said with a contented smile, "thank you very much."

— Chapter Six —

And Now, for Your Entertainment

At first Nathan thought they'd cross-dimensionalized back home. This new kingdom looked exactly like any major city in any major country. Towering buildings, masses of people, and traffic backed up for blocks. But it didn't take long to see that things were just a little bit different . . .

First there was the noise. Deafening. Like a thousand stereos and TVs all blaring at the same time.

Then there were the windows. Actually the lack of them. In place of windows there were . . . movie screens. That's right. Whether they were the windows in a taxi cab, the thousands of windows in a skyscraper, or the huge display windows of a department store, every pane of glass had been replaced by a motion picture screen. And every screen was playing a different movie! It was impossible to look anywhere without seeing at least twenty movies playing at the same time.

As a result, the people on the street barely moved. Why should they? What was happening on those screens, what was roaring in their ears, was a thousand times more interesting than real life. So they just stood and stared.

"What is this place?" Nathan shouted to his brother. But of course, Joshua couldn't hear. No one could hear. The noise was too deafening.

Just then they spotted a lone woman in rags. She seemed to be the only one moving as she pushed a dilapidated old cart down the street. They raced up to her.

"Excuse me, ma'am!" Josh shouted. "Could you tell us where we are?"

"The Kingdom of Entertainment!" she shouted back.

"I'm sorry, I can't hear you!" he yelled.

"THE KINGDOM OF ENTERTAINMENT!"

The boys looked at each other. They still couldn't make out her words.

Not surprised, she reached into her cart and brought out two sets of clear little balls, about the size of marbles. She handed a pair to each boy and motioned for them to put them in their ears. Figuring they had nothing to lose, they popped them inside. And suddenly they heard . . .

Silence. Blessed, beautiful silence.

"That will be 2,340 Jairkens," she said, holding out her hand for payment.

"I'm sorry," Nathan answered. "We don't, well we don't have any of those 'Jairker' things."

"No Jairkens!" she scorned. "Then give those back before I call the police!"

"But, without them . . ." Josh protested, "I mean, it's so noisy we can't even hear ourselves think."

"That's the whole idea!" a voice boomed from behind.

The boys spun around to see the Merchant of Emotions. He was projected upon the glass panes of a revolving door. His image flickered as the windows spun round and round and round. Behind him was the ever-faithful six-legged TeeBolt trying to sneak a peek at the boys.

The Merchant continued. "These people wanted entertainment, so I gave them entertainment. Nonstop, never-ceasing entertainment." He broke into a brief cackle. "Now they can never hear themselves think, or speak. And, of course, they'll never be able to hear Imager's voice. Their only relief is in buying silence—and that, my little friends, costs a pretty penny."

"I should say so," the street vendor complained. "And they've just stolen four minutes' worth."

"Put it on my tab," the Merchant chuckled.

"You have no tab," she argued. "And if I keep giving away silence I'll be so poor I'll never—"

Before she could finish, the Merchant reached for the Emotion Generator strapped to his chest and flipped a single switch. A cloud of mist shot out from a little nozzle and struck the vendor in her stomach. Suddenly she began to cry—uncontrollably. Deep, gut-wrenching sobs shook her entire body.

The boys looked on as she dropped to her knees and continued to weep hysterically.

"What did you do to her?" Joshua demanded.

"Oh, she's just feeling a little SENTIMENTAL."

"But how. . . ?" Nathan stammered.

"They don't call me the Merchant of Emotions for nothing."

"You mean you can control—"

"People's emotions," the Merchant pretended to yawn. "Yes, well, that's the whole idea now, isn't it. Would you care for a demonstration?"

"NO!" both brothers shouted in unison.

"Yes, well, we'll see," the Merchant smiled as he carefully looked them over. "So, Imager has sent you two worthless creatures to stop my attack upon his Upside-down Kingdom?"

"We're not worthless," Josh said, taking half a step closer. "We've been re-Breathed and we have our weapons."

"Yes, a bag of water and a rather ill-fitting suit of armor."

Nathan shifted slightly. The armor still felt too big.

"You must remind me to give you the name of my tailor. He could do wonders."

Josh had had enough. He started toward the revolving doors.

"Joshua!" Nathan shouted.

"Don't worry, he's just a reflection."

But Nathan was worried. He remembered all too well what the Merchant's sister had done to all three of them with her reflections.

Josh didn't care. As the brain and super-jock, he'd always had plenty of confidence (not to mention, ego). Perhaps a little too much. He continued forward—bold, courageous, and absolutely sure of himself.

"My, the Josh is a brave one, isn't he?" the Merchant chuckled.

Joshua ignored him and called back to Nathan. "Come on, he's just a stupid reflection."

The Merchant turned toward TeeBolt. "The Josh has bravery. Shall we see if he has anything else?"

TeeBolt jumped up on the Merchant in glee, which of course meant lots of panting and drooling. "Will you get down—get down!"

Josh took advantage of the distraction and raced for the door. He wasn't exactly sure what he was going to do when he got there, but his hand was already on the waterskin. He was already opening its lid.

But the Merchant was too fast. He spotted Joshua and reached down to the Generator.

"Josh! Look out!"

Too late. The Merchant flipped another switch and a cloud of mist struck Josh on the neck.

Suddenly the boy began to scream in terror.

"Josh, what is it?" Nathan shouted as he ran to him. "Joshua! Joshua!"

But Joshua couldn't speak. He could only scream and point to the ground. At first Nathan had no idea what Josh was pointing at—what was causing so much terror. And then he saw it.

An ant. A single, solitary ant was crossing the sidewalk in front of them.

Josh was beside himself. The screaming grew worse. He scampered to the wall and huddled against it, shaking like a leaf.

"Stop it!" Nathan shouted at the Merchant. "Whatever you're doing, stop it at once!"

The Merchant broke into even harsher laughter and spoke. But Nathan couldn't make out all of the words.

"You . . . no match . . . ha, ha, ha . . . will suffer . . . now end!"

The kingdom's noise had returned. It began to

drown out the other sounds. The little marbles of silence were wearing down.

Nate looked back to his brother. Joshua still seemed to be screaming, but he could no longer hear him. There was only blaring noise now. Nathan looked back to the Merchant. The creature still seemed to be laughing—as he reached for another switch on his chest. . . .

———

After a few more barks and yelps, the young doctor hopped back to his feet and continued down the hall with Denise. Naturally, he was a little embarrassed, but what other choice did he have? Denise had given him the order and Denise was the boss.

"What's your name?" she asked as they rounded the corner toward her mother's room.

"What would you like it to be?"

It didn't take long for her to have an answer. Now, Denny really wasn't trying to be mean—and she certainly wasn't in the habit of making fun of people. But the doctor had been so arrogant and such a know-it-all before that she couldn't resist the temptation to get even. And since there was no one there to stop her . . .

"Your name is . . . uh, Lame Brain. That's right, Dr. Lame Brain."

Without so much as a flinch, the doctor answered, "My name is Dr. Lame Brain."

Just then the elevator doors opened and two orderlies rushed out carrying an old man—the same one Denny had met when she stepped out of the limo. The toothless old gentleman who had jumped up and tried to click his heels. Only now he wasn't jumping. He wasn't even breathing.

Immediately the doctor was at his side. "What's wrong?"

"Heart attack!" the orderly shouted.

"Set him down," the doctor ordered. "Get a crash cart, stat! We have a code blue!"

"The crash carts are all busy," the first orderly cried. "The people are dropping like flies out there—everyone's overdoing it; they're all killing themselves!"

Without a word the doctor dropped to his knees and began CPR. He pinched the old man's nose and began breathing into his mouth.

"What's happening?" Denise cried. "What's going on?"

"Don't you see?" the doctor shouted as he turned from the man's mouth and began pumping his chest. "Without pain, no one knows their limits. Without pain, everyone will die."

The thought caught Denny off guard—but only for a second. If that was the only problem . . . and if she could control anything.

Quickly she brought up the Tablet and scrawled out two more words:

N-O D-E-A-T-H.

Suddenly the old man came back to life—coughing, wheezing, and looking around very wide-eyed. But he was alive, now. No doubt about it.

The doctor stared up at Denny, his own eyes widening in astonishment.

"Well," Denise grinned, "that should take care of that."

———

Back in Master Control another alarm sounded.

Aristophenix, Listro Q, Samson, and Mr. Hornsberry had all been watching Denise and the doctor on the main screen. They cringed when Denise made the doctor bark like a dog. They were embarrassed when she gave him the humiliating name. But now she was starting to use the Tablet for good. Now things were getting better. Or so they thought.

"Alarm, for what?" Listro Q asked. "By eliminating death, didn't a good thing she do?"

The Weaver shook his head angrily. "Punch up the future!" he shouted to an assistant. "Punch up two hundred years into the future."

The big screen flickered. Before them sat an incredibly old and outrageously fat queen. In fact, she was so huge that it took three thrones just to hold her. With all the wrinkles and rolls of fat, it was hard to recognize the face. But since this was Denise's Control Room, and since they were watching Denise, everyone had a pretty good idea who it was. She was so old and so fat she couldn't move. And yet she was sighing in pleasure. Incredible, indescribable pleasure. The reason soon became apparent. The Merchant of Emotions was standing right beside her. Her entire body was covered in his mists of emotions.

"Wide angle!" the Weaver called.

The picture on the screen grew wider. Now they could see Denise's thrones were in the middle of a desert. An endless desert surrounded by thick, putrid air. Air so dark that it was impossible to tell whether it was day or night. Millions of people crowded around her coughing and choking—trying to breathe but finding it impossible.

Samson looked at the screen and chattered a question.

The Weaver answered, "Without death Upside-Downers will overrun their kingdom and use up all its resources."

It was true. There were no trees or grass or even oceans—just people, billions and billions of swarming people. "Swarming" probably isn't the right word because to swarm you have to move. These people were so crowded together they couldn't move. All they could do was cough and choke . . . and plead.

"Please," they begged the gigantic Denise. "Please let us die. Have mercy on us, please let us die, please, please. . . ."

Those that still had arms and legs could no longer use them. Their bodies had simply worn out. Yet, they could not die. They were forced to live century after century.

They weren't in physical pain. Denise had never changed that order. Theirs was a different kind of pain. A pain of the mind. A torture of having to live hundreds of years. A torture of having to survive in this harsh, impossibly crowded world. A torture of knowing things would only get worse.

Aristophenix turned to the Weaver.

> You'll have to excuse me,
> I'm usually pretty clever.
> But is this what happens
> when Upside-Downers live forever?

The Weaver slowly nodded. "In the beginning, when Upside-Downers turned from Imager, he commanded me to weave Death into their world."

"This, because of?" Listro Q asked, motioning toward the screen.

Again the Weaver nodded. "To live forever in any

kingdom without Imager is impossibly cruel. Without Imager's rule, death is a gift, not a curse. Without Imager, death is mercy."

"But," Mr. Hornsberry cleared his throat, "why is Denise so phenomenally overweight and insensitive?"

"She's done away with all of life's struggles, yes she has. Without struggles, without hardships, she has grown fat and lazy."

"Laziness of her body," Listro Q commented.

"And of her mind," Aristophenix added.

"And most dangerous of all," the Weaver continued, "there is a fatness of her soul, a laziness of her spirit."

The group stood looking on in silence.

"Still," Mr. Hornsberry offered, "this is not necessarily the future. If Master Nathan and Joshua are successful in their attempts to stop the Merchant, this will all change."

The Weaver nodded. "*If* they can stop him."

Only the choking and moaning from the future filled the room. The Weaver could stand no more. "Go back to the present," he ordered. Once again the image on the screen flickered and changed.

Suddenly Samson began to chatter.

"Yes," the Weaver agreed, "in case Joshua and Nathan fail, a back-up plan would be good."

Again Samson spoke.

Again the Weaver agreed. "Because of your closeness to her, she *might* listen. But the risk of a non-Upside-Downer in this sort of situation is—"

Samson cut him off with another burst of chatter.

"I understand your devotion, but even if you did go, she still doesn't understand you. She'd need a translator."

"Us you have," Listro Q offered.

"No, the risk of more than one non-Upside-Downer there is too great."

"That's a pity," Aristophenix sighed.

"Yes," Listro Q agreed. "Somebody else from Upside-down Kingdom we—" Suddenly his eyes landed on Mr. Hornsberry. "A minute wait!"

The dog shifted uncomfortably. "What?"

"From the Upside-down Kingdom, someone we need . . ."

"So . . ."

Aristophenix also saw it. He turned toward Hornsberry. "Of course, someone of great courage . . ."

The Weaver joined in. "Someone of great intelligence . . ."

"And wisdom," Listro Q added.

"Of course." Aristophenix smiled at Mr. Hornsberry. "Now, who do you suppose that someone could be?"

Mr. Hornsberry swallowed nervously. As the only other citizen from the Upside-down Kingdom, he had a feeling they'd already selected that "someone."

"I would be happy to volunteer," he nervously hedged, "most happy, indeed. However, if you recall, back home I am merely a stuffed animal. Once you return me to the Upside-down Kingdom, I'm afraid I shall once again—"

"I could adjust your weave," the Weaver offered. "Temporarily, you understand."

"That would be most kind, however . . ."

The group looked in eager anticipation.

"That is to say . . ."

They continued to wait.

Mr. Hornsberry gave a nervous cough.

Still they waited.

"Oh, very well," he snapped. "If anyone's cut out to save the day, I suppose it is myself."

"All right, Mr. Hornsberry!" The group cheered and slapped him on the back. "What a guy! What a hero!"

"Yes, well, that goes without saying now, doesn't it."

"You'll need this." The Weaver suddenly produced another Cross-Dimensionalizer (as if he knew Mr. Hornsberry was going to volunteer all along). "You must do your best to convince Denise to destroy the Tablet. She must return everything to the original weave. Do you understand?"

Samson and Mr. Hornsberry nodded.

Without another word the Weaver hung the Cross-Dimensionalizer around Mr. Hornsberry's neck, stooped down to punch the four buttons,

Beep . . .

Bop . . .

Burp . . .

Bleep . . .

and they were gone.

— CHAPTER SEVEN —

A CLOSE CALL

"I say, this is rather odd!" Mr. Hornsberry exclaimed as he looked around the enormous room with its towering walls, full-length windows, and sparkling chandeliers. "Do you have the slightest idea where we might be?"

Samson fired back a reply. It was long and loud. But no matter how long or loud, the answer was still your basic . . . "Nope."

Mr. Hornsberry started to trot around the room, carefully investigating it. "Apparently it is some sort of mansion—a palace by all appearances. Yet, what would Denise be doing in such a residence? And what is that irritating ruckus outside?"

Beyond the windows they could hear an angry crowd shouting and yelling. Before they could investigate, a giant door at the far end of the room slid open and a stuffy butler appeared. He was stiff, snooty and, if possible, even more snobbish than Mr. Hornsberry. "May I help you?" the man inquired.

"That is your reason for employment, is it not?" Mr. Hornsberry asked, trying to sound even more haughty. (After all, he had his reputation to uphold.) "Be a good fellow, now. Run along and fetch Miss Denise. We'd like to speak with her."

"I beg your pardon, but whom, or shall I say, what is calling?"

Mr. Hornsberry coughed slightly. The butler was better than he had expected. But before he could fire off a comeback, Samson started to buzz the man's head. The butler remained unimpressed. Instead, he simply turned for the door.

"I don't believe we've dismissed you," Mr. Hornsberry called.

"Actually," the butler answered as he tried to swat Samson aside, "I was about to procure some bug spray."

Samson squealed in panic.

"You're crazy!" Mr. Hornsberry cried. Then catching himself, he continued a bit more sophisticatedly. "That is to say, I see no purpose in such barbaric actions."

"And while I'm at it, I think I shall call the Dog Pound. Talking animals can be such a nuisance."

"You'll do nothing of the kind." Denise suddenly appeared at the door behind the butler. Well, at least they thought it was Denise. Instead of her usual baggy pants and jean jacket, this Denise was decked out in a riding habit complete with riding whip and derby. "These folks are my friends," she continued. "You will treat them with the respect they deserve."

"Miss Denise!" Mr. Hornsberry cried. He quickly trotted toward her, being careful to turn up his nose as he passed the butler.

Denny couldn't help but giggle. "That will be all, Chauncy."

"As you wish, Miss Denise." The butler turned, but fired one last comment to Mr. Hornsberry. "Try not to shed on the furniture. Dog hair can be *so* loathsome."

For the briefest second Mr. Hornsberry wanted to sink his teeth deep into the man's calf. The fellow wanted "loathsome"—that would show him "loathsome." But the dog managed to fight back his instincts. After all, he still had his reputation to uphold.

Meanwhile, Samson began playfully dive-bombing Denny's head.

"Hey, fella!" Denise giggled, trying to fight him off. "Cut it out. Come on now, knock it off. Stop it."

And just that fast, Samson fell to the ground, unable to fly.

"SAMMY!" Denise dropped to her knees. "Are you OK?"

"What happened?" Mr. Hornsberry cried.

"I don't know, I just . . . Oh, of course, I get it."

"Get what?"

"Well, I have this thing to write on." She held up the Tablet. "And whatever I write on it happens."

"Yes, we're quite aware of that fact."

"Well, one of the things I wrote was that people have to obey me."

"I fail to see how—"

"I told Sammy to stop bothering me, and he had to stop."

Samson chattered a terse reply.

"Sorry, little guy," Denise laughed, "but around

here, I'm the boss. However," she said, pretending to sound very official, "you now have my permission to fly again."

Samson took off and began giving Denise the lecture of her life, though this time he was careful to keep his distance.

"What's he so bothered about?" Denise complained. "I said I was sorry."

Samson continued to chatter, but Mr. Hornsberry didn't translate. He figured it was best to let the little guy cool off a bit. Instead, he had a few questions of his own. "Would you mind telling me why you are wearing such costly clothes?"

"Oh," Denise chuckled, giving her riding whip a couple of slaps on her leg. "When you can have anything you want, it's kinda hard not to go for the best."

"Yes, well, I'm afraid that's one of the reasons the Weaver has sent us."

"Cool!" Denise exclaimed.

"He knows all about the Tablet."

"So he's sent you guys to thank me for all the good I'm doing."

"Well, not exact—"

"I mean these clothes and this palace—anybody could wish for these. But it took somebody special like me to do all the good stuff, didn't it?"

Samson chattered off a sharp reply.

Mr. Hornsberry carefully translated, "Not exactly. You see, in your admirable efforts to transform the world to a superior status, it appears you are actually destroying it."

Denise was shocked. "No way! I'm making this world a *better* place—better than Imager ever did!"

Samson chattered his most stinging comment yet.

"Sure I am," Denise argued. She didn't have to wait for the translation. " 'Course not everyone understands it's for the best, but they will."

"Not everyone?" Mr. Hornsberry asked.

"Don't you hear them? All that shouting and screaming outside?"

"That is directed toward you?"

Denise nodded and crossed to a giant pair of balcony doors. As she threw them open, the shouting and screaming grew much louder.

"They want me to bring pain back into the world, can you believe it?"

*   Mr. Hornsberry and Samson moved to the balcony for a better look. Below were thousands of people all shaking their fists and yelling. And for good reason. Their bodies were twisted and disfigured beyond belief. Hundreds were doubled over with disease or sprawled out on the lawn unable to walk. Many looked as if they should have been dead. But, of course, that was no longer possible.

"A few even want me to bring death back." Denise shook her head in amazement.

"But my dear Denise. Death . . . Pain . . . they're all part of Imager's plan. Don't you see how you're ruining his Tapestry?"

"No way!" Denise bristled. "I'm making things better."

Samson darted back and forth, chattering angrily.

Mr. Hornsberry translated. "Imager knows what's best. You've ignored his plans—you've changed the rules."

"Rules!" Denise exclaimed. "That's the whole problem! His rules were wrong!"

"And yours are better?" Mr. Hornsberry asked, referring to the shouting mob below.

Denny started to answer, then stopped. As she looked down to the people, her mind began to race. "Hmmm . . . you might be on to something."

Mr. Hornsberry and Samson glanced at each other. They didn't know what "something" Denise was thinking, but they had a pretty good idea her "something" wasn't exactly the same as their "something."

"Maybe that's the problem," she finally said. "Maybe there are too many rules altogether. Mine . . . Imager's. Maybe you're right. Maybe the real reason they're unhappy is because of all the rules."

"Miss Denise," Mr. Hornsberry tried to interrupt, "I did not mean to infer—"

"No one's ever let them do what they want to do."

"Miss Denise—"

"I mean, if you really want people to be happy, then you got to let them do their own thing." She was growing more and more excited. "Of course—that's it!"

"Miss Denise, Imager has laid down some very specific—"

But Denny no longer listened. She picked up the Tablet and started to write.

"What are you doing—what are you writing?"

Samson hovered over her shoulder for a closer look.

"Imager's got all these rules, right? *Do this, don't do that.* No wonder nobody's happy. What do we need all the rules for?"

Before Mr. Hornsberry could respond, she supplied her own answer. "We don't. To really be happy we should only have to do what WE want. To live the way WE want to."

She flipped the board around. There were only two words written on it:

N-O R-U-L-E-S.

Immediately, the people below the balcony broke into a rage. "Let's get her! Let's get the Tablet! Let's get the Tablet!" The entire crowd picked up the chant: "GET THE TABLET, GET THE TABLET, GET THE TABLET."

They began banging on the door. "GET THE TAB-LET, GET . . ."

"Knock it off!" Denise shouted. "I command you to stop!"

But they continued pounding on the door. "GET THE TABLET, GET THE TABLET, GET THE TAB-LET . . ."

"I thought they had to obey you!" Mr. Hornsberry shouted.

"They do! I don't under—" Then she broke into a sheepish grin. "Not anymore! I just wrote that there are no rules, remember? They don't have to obey me; they don't have to obey anyone!"

"GET THE TABLET, GET THE TABLET, GET THE TABLET . . ."

"If that's the case," Mr. Hornsberry shouted, "might I inquire if you have an alternate entrance?"

"Sure do, lots."

"GET THE TABLET! GET THE TABLET!"

"Then may I suggest we use one for a rather hasty retreat?"

Denise glanced down to the crowd just as they broke through the front door and started swarming into the mansion. "Good point, Hornsey!"

———

In the Kingdom of Entertainment the Merchant's image still flickered in the revolving doors, and Joshua was still huddled against the building, screaming. The Merchant had hit him with the mist of TERROR and was now taking aim at Nathan.

"Joshua . . . Joshua!" Nathan shouted. But it did no good. He looked up from his screaming brother just in time to see the Merchant flip another switch. Once again a cloud of vapor shot from the creature's Emotion Generator. Only this time it was heading for Nathan. The boy struggled to raise his heavy shield and block the mist, but he was too late. It hit him dead center in the chest.

Yet nothing happened. Unlike Joshua, there were no out-of-control feelings. No all-consuming emotions. Nothing.

A puzzled Nathan looked down. Sure enough, there was the mist. Sure enough, it had hit him smack dab in the chest. But not so sure enough, nothing happened. Why?

Then he saw it. The mist wasn't touching him; it was touching his armor. That clunky armor he'd had to haul around all this time had finally served a purpose. But not for long. For even as he looked, Nathan could see the tiny droplets of moisture eating their way through the metal, turning it to a liquid goo, working its way closer and closer to his body.

He spun back to his brother. "Joshua! Joshua, can you hear me?!"

But Joshua was too busy screaming for his life to hear anything. Not that he could anyway. The marbles of silence had worn off, and now there was only the roar from the kingdom's speakers and movie screens.

The Merchant fired off another cloud of mist. This time Nathan was fast enough to block it with his shield. But when it hit the shield, the metal of the shield also started to dissolve.

Nathan turned and ran.

The Merchant's body shook with laughter. "Up-side-Downers are such cowards," he cried. But his laughter soon stopped. The boy wasn't running away. He was running to the vendor's cart of marbles.

Nathan reached in and grabbed four more little balls. He quickly slipped two into his ears and rushed back to Josh with the other pair.

"What are you doing?" the Merchant cried. He reached down to his Generator and fired off two more clouds of mist. Nathan was too busy to raise his shield and both volleys hit him on the right side.

But he wasn't concerned. Not about those hits. He was concerned about the first one. The mist from it had finally eaten through his armor. Already he could feel its wetness touch his chest, and with that wetness came an uncontrollable emotion . . . WORRY. Worry about everything. Joshua, Denise, friends, school . . . He even began to worry about worrying. He knew none of it was real. He knew it all came from the Merchant. But he also knew he couldn't stop it.

He dropped to his knees. "This is not happening!" he screamed. But it did no good, except to make the Merchant of Emotions laugh louder.

"You think that's something!" he roared. "Wait till those other emotions get to you."

Frantically Nathan looked to his side. The other emotions were quickly eating through his armor just as the first had.

"NO!" he screamed, trying to fight the WORRY. "NOOOO!"

The Merchant continued to laugh.

"NO! NO! NO!" Nathan screamed, but it did no

good. The emotion was too strong to fight. In a last act of desperation he began to cry: "IMAGER PROMISED WE WOULD WIN! IMAGER PROMISED!!!"

And with that cry, the strangest thing happened. As Nathan shouted, as he claimed Imager's promise, the mist of WORRY began to evaporate. Nathan could actually feel the dampness start to leave his chest. And as it left, so did the WORRY.

"IMAGER PROMISED!" he continued to shout. "WE WILL WIN!"

The boy glanced down. To his amazement not only was the moisture evaporating from his chest but the hole in his breastplate began to seal up. The metal was actually healing itself, becoming as smooth and shiny as if it had never been pierced. He looked to his right side. The same was happening there. Then to his shield. The same.

What had the Weaver said ... *"The armor and shield are your belief—your protection?"* That was it! They were his belief! They were his trust in Imager! Somehow as he shouted the promise, he had activated that power, he had ignited that belief.

Nathan looked back down. Now the armor was as good as new. Slowly he rose to his feet and turned to the Merchant. It looked like it was time for a little showdown.

It was also time for the Merchant to panic. He fired off another round of emotion. Then another. But Nathan blocked them easily with his shield. As each hit, they hissed loudly and evaporated.

"What has the Nathan done? What has it done to my emotions?"

Nathan knelt back down to his brother, who was still screaming in fear. Quickly he shoved the marbles

of silence into his ears. "Josh, Josh, you got to listen to me! Joshua!" But Joshua was too overwhelmed with terror. Then Nathan spotted it. The mist the Merchant had fired at Josh. It was on his neck, glistening brightly in the sunlight.

Ever so gently, Nathan reached out and touched that mist with his armored glove. It hissed viciously and evaporated into steam.

"What . . . what happened?" Josh asked, shaking his head, trying to get his bearings. The TERROR he had felt was completely gone.

"It's the Merchant, over there at the doors. He was controlling you with—"

They turned to the revolving doors but the Merchant was no longer there. He had disappeared. Fortunately, that wasn't the only thing missing.

"Look!" Josh cried. He pointed to the glass windows in the building, then to every building. "The movie screens—they're gone. All of 'em! They're back to being just windows again!"

"And the noise," Nathan added. "It's also gone!"

The boys pulled the marbles of silence from their ears and looked around. Things were peaceful. Quiet. Well, as peaceful and quiet as any big city can be . . . if you don't count the honking horns, the squealing brakes, and shouting people.

"He's not here!" Joshua cried. "He's left for another kingdom."

The brothers shared frightened looks. Both knew what the other was thinking.

Josh grabbed his pocket Cross-Dimensionalizer and shouted into it. "Listro Q! Listro Q, you have to get us to earth—quick!"

"At your home, he is not yet," the answer came

through the unit. "One more kingdom, first he is visiting."

"Then send us there—we have to stop him!"

"Got it, I do," came the answer. Again the boys looked to each other. Neither was sure what was next. They had nearly lost the first battle. Hopefully they'd be ready for the next.

Then came the very familiar sounds:

Beep . . .
Bop . . .
Burp . . .
Bleep . . .

— CHAPTER EIGHT —

THE
OUT-OF-TIMERS

"*Now* where are we?" Nathan whined.

At first glance it looked like some kind of over-grown park. But a very weird overgrown park. There were lots of trees, but they were all perfectly straight, and they had no branches. They were planted in single file and covered with ivy. Below them were overgrown paths of concrete that stretched for as far as the eye could see. And on those paths were . . . Could it be? Yes. They were cars. Broken-down, rusted-out cars. Hundreds of them. Which meant those concrete lanes weren't pathways at all, but streets. And the branch-less trees in straight lines? What else but telephone poles!

Then there were the people. . . .

They were sitting inside the cars and on top of them. And they were all talking. Like the cars and the rest of the kingdom, they were dirty and in disrepair. Hair messed, faces unshaven, all sporting the latest in worn and tattered clothing.

Then there was the smell. *Their* smell. It was so strong it made the back of the boys' noses tickle. It was a safe bet that soap and water wasn't something this kingdom had discovered yet. Or if it had, then like the streets, cars, and telephone poles, its citizens simply didn't care to use it anymore.

And, speaking of "not caring," no one seemed too surprised when the brothers suddenly cross-dimensionalized in front of them.

"Excuse me," Josh called to a nearby car. Its doors had rusted off and it was filled with a handful of older folks. "Excuse me, could you tell us where we are?"

At first no one bothered to answer. They just continued their chitchat.

"Excuse me!"

Finally a ragged man from the front seat shouted, "We can't tell you where you *are,* but we can tell you where you *arrived.*"

Josh threw a look to Nate. "I'm sorry, what?"

"We were Out-of-Timers."

"Out-of-Timers?" Josh asked.

"That *was* correct. We *were* Out-of-Timers."

Again the boys traded glances. It was Nathan's turn. "What do you mean, *were?* What are you now?"

"We had no *now.* Nor will we have one in the future."

"What?" Nathan exclaimed.

"What do you mean, 'you have no *now*'?" Josh asked.

The man turned to the group in the backseat. "I had forgotten how stupid youth was." The others chuckled and clucked their tongues in agreement. The old man turned back to Joshua. "We neither had a *now* in the past nor will we have a *now* in the future. We will think only of our past or of our future. We have not lived nor will we ever live in the *now*."

Nathan turned to his brother. "You're the brain. What's he saying?"

"I'm not exactly sure," Josh scowled. "But I think he's saying these people don't have a present."

"What?"

"It sounds like they can remember the past OK. And they can think about the future. . . . But they don't have a now."

"They don't have a now?" Nathan repeated.

Josh nodded. "They can't enjoy the present."

"That's awful!"

"It *was* awful," the old man agreed. "And it *will be* awful."

"Who is responsible for this?" Joshua demanded.

"There never was an *is* nor will there be an *is*."

"All right, all right, who *was* responsible for this?"

A beggar from the backseat spoke up. "The creature with the six-legged pet—the creature with all the emotions."

"The Merchant!" Nathan cried. "Then he's here!"

"He *was* here. And he *will be* here, but—"

"I know, I know," Nathan sighed, "but there is no *is*."

The second beggar nodded with satisfaction. The group continued speaking of the past, recalling how the Merchant had cast his spell—how he had stolen their now—how they could only have feelings for the past or the future.

Josh listened patiently, but it wasn't long before he

broke in. "Don't you guys want to do something? Don't you want to fight to get those *now* feelings back?"

"Oh, we had tried in the past," the first beggar explained. "And we'll try in the future—"

"But *now!*" Josh exclaimed. "What about *now?*"

"There was and will be no *now.*"

"Don't you see?" Josh sputtered in frustration. "The future will always become the *now.* And then you won't be able to do anything because it's *now.*"

The group in the car looked at him blankly. He tried again. "You will never do anything, because when you do it, it will no longer be the future, but it will be the present."

The group shrugged and turned back to their conversation.

"Doesn't anyone care?!"

There was no answer.

"OK, OK." Josh tried to stay calm. "Just tell us where he is . . . no, no, I mean just tell us where he *was* going?"

"Into that swamp!" a woman from the front seat shouted. "When they heard you had arrived, the two of them raced into that swamp."

Joshua and Nathan turned in the direction she pointed. Not far away stretched a huge swamp, so large it could have been a small sea. It was covered with thick vegetation and shrouded in a dark, impenetrable fog.

"In there?" Nathan asked nervously.

"That's right!" the second beggar shouted. "They ran in there and someday we will follow."

The other passengers nodded and continued recalling the past and dreaming of what they would do in the future.

"Come on," Josh motioned to Nathan, "let's get him."

"In there?" Nathan repeated.

"Come on!"

"By ourselves?"

"I don't see any volunteers, now come on!" With that Joshua turned and headed for the swamp.

Nathan hesitated a moment. He turned back to the car and swallowed hard. "You sure nobody wants to help?"

"Yes, we will help," the first beggar repeated. "Someday, very soon, we will help."

Nathan let out a heavy sigh as he realized "someday" would never arrive. He turned to join his brother, his armor clunking with every step. Strange, the heavy metal suit fit a lot better since their first encounter with the Merchant. Nathan wondered if he'd grown a bit. And the shield didn't seem nearly so heavy.

But the swamp still looked very, very dark. . . .

———

Back at Master Control one alarm sounded after another.

"What's she doing now!" the Weaver cried in frustration. "Put her on the screen!"

An assistant brought another image to the center screen. In it Denise, Mr. Hornsberry, and Samson were running toward a beach. Behind them was an angry mob, screaming: "GET THE TABLET, GET THE TABLET, GET THE TABLET!"

"Close in on Denise!" the Weaver called. "Let's hear what she's saying!"

The assistant obeyed as Aristophenix and Listro Q leaned forward for a better listen. . . .

"Hurry!" Denise shouted as they arrived at the beach and started through the sand. "The beach people will protect us. See! Look how happy they are!"

Unlike the wretched souls pursuing them, the crowd on the beach was having a great time.

"See!" Denny cried. "Not everybody hates what I've done."

Mr. Hornsberry and Samson did see—actually they saw too much. Hundreds were staggering around. Some drunk, some on drugs. Others were out of control, screaming, partying, beating on each other, and . . . well, if you could name it they were probably doing it . . . and worse!

Mr. Hornsberry shouted over the din, "Although I am incredibly bright, I fail to understand what has transpired."

Samson chattered an agreement.

"It was your idea!" Denise shouted.

"Mine?"

"You said the one thing I forgot. The one thing to make a perfect kingdom."

"Which is. . . ?"

She dodged a couple beer bottles flying in their direction and continued. "If you really want people to be happy, then let them do their own thing!"

"No rules!" Mr. Hornsberry shouted.

"That's right," Denise cried. "Look!"

She pointed to a city bus that roared past. Apparently the driver wanted to go to the beach, so he was going to the beach. The passengers inside didn't look too crazy about the idea, but if this is what he wanted, they had little say in the matter.

"Looks like there are a few glitches to work out," Denise shrugged.

Before Mr. Hornsberry could agree, they came upon two parents pleading with their little five-year-old. Actually, she wasn't so little. In fact, she was as wide as she was tall, and for good reason. She was cramming her mouth with so much chocolate she could barely breathe. It was all over her mouth, her face, her entire body. And still she continued to eat, nearly choking as she shoved in one candy bar after another.

Spotting Denise, the father raced to her and begged, "Please, make her stop. Look what she's doing to herself!"

"I'm sorry," Denise sympathized, "but she has the right to do what she wants. At least she's having a good time."

"GET THE TABLET! GET THE TABLET! GET THE TABLET!"

She looked back over her shoulder. The angry mob, the thousands of broken and twisted people, was starting to gain on them. "We gotta keep going!" she shouted.

As they continued forward, another group joined their side. Young people. Very angry young people. "We got to talk to you!" they demanded. "We got to talk to you *now*!"

"What's wrong?" Denise shouted.

"It's the radio stations," a blond boy cried. "They've gone off the air 'cause nobody wants to work!"

"If that's what they want," Denise argued, "then they ought to be able to—"

"It's not just the radio stations," an older girl complained. "The grocery stores are closed, the malls. We can't even rent a movie."

"That's right," a studious boy with glasses jumped in. "And what about the hospitals and the doctors and—"

"I'm sorry, guys, but if that's what people want—"

"But we don't want it!" they shouted. "Don't you get it? We don't want any of this!"

Suddenly there was a loud honking. They spun around to see that the city bus had returned . . . and it was heading directly for them!

"LOOK OUT!" everyone screamed.

Denise dove to the ground as the bus roared past. It missed her by only a few feet. The young people at her side weren't so lucky. It careened into them, knocking them down and running over them. But thanks to Denny's Tablet, they weren't dead and they felt no pain—their bodies were just smashed and destroyed.

The bus plowed into a hot-dog stand, wiping out another dozen or so people, then veered sharply, and finally flipped over, trapping all the riders inside. Everyone was shouting. Panicking. Screaming hysterically. Suddenly the engine caught fire and began spewing thick black smoke. Any minute it looked as if the entire bus would burst into flames.

Passengers tried to break out their windows but couldn't. They pressed their faces against the glass, banging on it, begging for help, pleading for someone to come to their rescue.

No one did.

Lifeguards simply turned over on their blankets for a better view. A policeman quit his volleyball game and watched with interest. Others pressed in to enjoy the spectacle as the black smoke filled the bus, and panic surged.

Denise was beside herself. "ISN'T ANYBODY GOING TO HELP?"

"And ruin the show?" an elderly woman asked as she adjusted her beach chair to see better. "Why should we care?"

" 'CAUSE THEY'RE GOING TO DIE!"

"People don't die anymore, remember?" the boy with the glasses said with a grin.

"WHAT ABOUT THEIR PAIN?"

"Wrong again," the father laughed. "There is no pain."

Denise was outraged. "YOU'RE JUST GOING TO SIT THERE AND LET THE BUS BLOW UP!?"

"Should be fun!" the elderly woman nodded.

Others agreed. "Do your own thing!" someone shouted. "That's right!" another cried.

All of this as, inside the bus, one person after another was overcome with smoke and slid from the windows.

Denise was in a panic. She had to do something. But what? This wasn't the kingdom she wanted. Nothing was turning out like she thought.

She looked at the Tablet in her hand. It was scratched from the fall, but her commands were still written in ink—impossible to erase. But why would she want to? If she changed those commands, it would mean she was wrong and Imager was right. And she still wasn't convinced of that. Not yet. Not completely.

— CHAPTER NINE —

THE INVITATION

"Josh . . . Josh where are you?"

"Over here."

"Where?"

"Right over—ouch! That's my foot!"

"Sorry."

"Ow!"

"Now what?"

"That's my other foot!"

It was dark in the swamp. Real dark. So dark that the brothers couldn't see a thing, not even themselves.

"This is impossible," Nathan complained as they waded through the thick, smelly ooze. The muck clung and tugged at their every step. Then, of course, there was the dense undergrowth of branches that kept slapping them in the face. "How are we supposed to find the Merchant if we can't even see where we—"

"Shh . . . listen."

"I don't hear any—"

"Shhhhh . . ."

Nathan did his best to keep still. Not an easy trick when you're waist deep in muck, when it's so dark you can't see, and when you happen to be the World's All-Time Champion Whiner. Yet, with his greatest effort, Nate was able to hold off complaining for nearly ten seconds—a new personal record. Then he heard it, too. "What is it?"

"Sounds like . . . panting," Josh whispered.

"Like a giant dog," Nathan agreed. "Like . . ."

They both had the same answer. "TeeBolt!"

"That means we're right on top of 'em," Nathan whispered.

"But where?"

They heard a faint click that sounded like a switch being flipped. Then the gentle sound of mist falling. Just as quickly, Josh started to whimper, "How come Imager gave *you* that suit of armor?"

"What. . . ?"

"It's not fair, you *always* get the good stuff."

"What are you talking about?" Nathan whispered.

"It's just like at home. Mom and Dad always treat you better—"

"Josh—"

"—just 'cause you're the baby."

"What's wrong with you?" Nathan demanded. "Josh . . . Joshua?"

There was a faint chuckle just a few feet away. Nathan's blood went cold. There was no mistaking its owner.

"Sounds like the Joshua is feeling a little JEAL-OUS," the Merchant's voice taunted. This was followed by more sounds of panting and slurping—obviously from the giant six-legged pet.

"You always get what you want," Joshua continued to complain.

"Josh," Nathan whispered, "where are you?"

"Just 'cause of that stupid hip of yours—"

"It's the Merchant—he's controlling your emotions—where did he spray you?"

"—everyone's always feeling sorry for you."

Nathan reached toward Josh's voice. He tried to grab him, but only caught his shirt sleeve and the waterskin hanging around his neck.

Josh pulled back. "Get away!" The shirt sleeve slipped through Nate's armored fingers. So did the waterskin. But not before his sharp metal glove ripped a gash into the top of it.

"Now look what you've—"

But that was as far as Josh got before the glow stopped him. The glow of the water. In the utter blackness the liquid spilling from the tear gave off a faint light.

"It's Imager's words!" the Merchant cried as he covered his eyes. "Put it away! Put it away!"

Both boys had used Imager's liquid words and letters before. Both had seen its incredible power at work. But neither had seen the liquid in the dark. Neither knew that it glowed. Not a lot, mind you, but just enough to see each other, the nearby Merchant, his pet . . . and the moisture of emotion glistening on Josh's left shoulder.

The Merchant stumbled backward, shielding his eyes as if the faint glow were blazing. "TeeBolt, quickly! Come!" He turned and waded deeper into the swamp. The giant dog splashed after him. "Not so close, you nincompoop! Not so close!"

"Josh," Nathan called as he reached toward the moisture on his brother's shoulder, "let me touch that and—"

"Look how you ripped my waterskin!" Josh whimpered. "It's no fair. Your stuff always lasts longer than—"

Finally Nathan laid his hand on his brother's shoulder . . . right on top of the moisture. There was a loud hiss as the emotion boiled away and Joshua's senses suddenly returned.

They looked up just in time to see TeeBolt follow his master into the thick mist. Now that Josh was back in control he shouted, "Let's go! We have to stop them before they leave for earth!"

"But how?" Nathan argued. "We can't see a thing."

"We got this water for our light. Come on!"

"But those emotions! They nearly had you!"

"Just keep fighting them off with that armor! You're doin' great."

"Yeah, but—"

"You defend us with your armor. I'll use the water to light our way. C'mon!"

Before Nathan could argue any further, Josh started into the darkness. He held out the waterskin, trying not to let any more spill from its torn opening, but using its glow to guide their steps.

It wasn't long before they spotted the Merchant. As usual, he was arguing with TeeBolt as they both stumbled and staggered in the impenetrable darkness. "No!" the Merchant shouted. "*You're* the pet. *I'm* the master. You go first!"

TeeBolt whined, panted, and slobbered in protest.

"Merchant!" Joshua shouted.

The Merchant spun around. For the first time since they met, they saw fear on his face. "Get away!" he shouted, shielding his eyes against the light of the words. "Keep that water away from me!"

"Oh, so this makes you a little nervous, does it?" Josh asked, holding the water out a bit farther.

"Josh," Nathan warned, "be careful."

"That's right," the Merchant threatened as he reached to the Emotion Generator strapped to his chest. "Come any closer and I'll fire."

"We're not afraid of you," Joshua said as he continued to slosh forward in the swamp.

"Have it your way," the Merchant sneered as he flipped another switch.

"Look out!" Nathan cried. Before he knew it he found himself leaping in front of Josh to block the mist with his shield. It struck the metal and let out a violent hiss.

"Thanks," Josh grinned. "You're getting pretty good at that!"

Nathan grinned back, a little nervous and a lot amazed at his newfound courage.

"Keep your distance," the Merchant warned. "Stay away with that water!"

It was all starting to make sense now—everything Imager and the Weaver had said. The boys each had their weapons. Nathan, his armor and shield—Joshua, his water. If they worked together, maybe they could defeat the Merchant. They started toward the creature.

The Merchant backed up and began firing one emotion after another. But with Josh's light Nathan could see the clouds of mist coming. He raised his shield and blocked each and every one as they hit the metal and evaporated with a sinister hiss.

"TeeBolt!" the Merchant cried. "Attack!"

But TeeBolt was too busy running in the other direction to worry about attacking.

"TeeBolt!"

The brothers continued forward. Josh held the water out farther and farther. "Would you like a little drink?"

The Merchant began to tremble. "The Joshua must keep that away. The Joshua does not know its power!"

Neither boy was surprised at the Merchant's fear. They remembered all too well how the water had destroyed his evil sister's kingdom of Seerlo.

Josh adjusted the rip at the top of the waterskin so even more light shone out. The faint glow seemed to blind the Merchant. He covered his eyes and cried, "Please . . . please have mercy. . . ."

They continued forward. Finally they stood directly over him. The Merchant began to cower, to shake like a frightened puppy. Josh raised the glowing liquid above the creature's head.

"No, please . . . I'll do anything the Joshua asks—please, please."

"Anything?"

"Yes, yes . . ."

"You'll return to your own world? You'll leave the Upside-down Kingdom alone?"

"Put it away, please—"

"You'll leave the Upside-down Kingdom alone??"

———

The smoke victims in the bus had all collapsed and still no one had moved to help. Instead, the crowd started complaining that the bus hadn't caught fire.

"You're the reason!" they shouted at Denise. "It's your fault! You stopped the show!"

"No . . ." Denise stammered as she backed away.

"Boring!" they screamed. "You are boring!"

"It's not true. I've made things better."

Suddenly she heard other voices. "GET THE TAB-LET! GET THE TABLET! GET THE TABLET!" She twirled around to see the first group that had been chasing her from the mansion. They had finally caught up and were closing in.

Others joined the crowd. The father with the choc-olate-covered daughter. The young people who had been hit by the bus. Some walked, others staggered, and many dragged themselves toward her. "You've made our lives a nightmare!" they shouted. "You must be stopped!" You are *evil*. EVIL!"

"No, I've created good!" Denise cried.

"EVIL, EVIL, EVIL . . ."

"GET THE TABLET, GET THE TABLET, GET THE TABLET . . ."

Denny tried to run but it was no use. They came at her from every side. Frustrated, angry, twisted and ruined people.

"BORING, BORING . . ."

"EVIL, EVIL . . ."

"GET THE TABLET, GET THE TABLET . . ."

"Mr. Hornsberry, Samson—do something! Help me!"

But there was nothing they could do.

"Don't you understand?!" Denise shouted as the circle closed in tighter and tighter. "I've made things better!"

"You've made our lives boring!" a drug-crazed girl screamed.

"Unspeakable!" a burn victim cried.

"Unlivable!" a twisted creature shrieked. "You must be stopped!"

They were nearly on top of her now. Denise pulled the Tablet closer. "NO!" she cried. "DON'T YOU SEE . . . I JUST, I JUST WANT EVERYBODY TO—"

Suddenly, she had an idea. She reached for her pen.

"Stop her!" the father screamed.

The crowd lunged at her, but not before Denny finished writing. "I just want everybody to . . ." She spun the Tablet around to reveal the words:

F-E-E-L G-O-O-D!

The Merchant of Emotions let out a screeching laugh. "TOO LATE!" he screamed into the boys' faces. "YOU'RE TOO LATE!"

He vanished. Instantly. Without a trace. Except for the giant six-legged pet who started whining at being left behind.

Back in Master Control, alarms and lights flashed everywhere.

"What's happening?" Aristophenix cried.

"Wrong, what's?" Listro Q yelled.

"Denise has given the invitation!" the Weaver shouted back.

"What?"

"She's invited the Merchant of Emotions to the Upside-down Kingdom!"

— CHAPTER TEN —

ROUND ONE

A shadow fell across the angry mob. They looked from Denise to the sky as a huge leather-winged creature blocked the sun and dove directly for them.

"Look out!" they cried. "It's coming at us!"

They spun from Denise and started to run. But they'd only taken a few steps before the Merchant of Emotions swooped down and gently landed between them and the girl.

"Please," he called, "I mean the Upside-Downers no harm. I must speak to the Upside-Downers. Please. PLEASE!"

The crowd slowly came to a stop and turned. They had no idea what an "Upside-Downer" was, but the creature seemed pretty sincere. And since he wasn't gobbling up any of them or blasting them away with ray guns, they figured he might be an OK alien. It might even be safe to stick around and hear what he said.

The Merchant folded his wings, patiently preened the crystal scales on his back, and waited. The more curious members of the crowd took a step or two closer. Others followed. The Merchant continued to clean. Then, when he was sure he had everyone's attention, he spoke. "Hi, there."

The crowd gasped and jumped back.

"Please, I am here to help." He tried to look friendly and smile—not an easy job when you have a beak for a mouth.

The people murmured among themselves. Finally the father of the candy-bar eater stepped forward. "Who are you?" he asked, trying to sound courageous. Of course, he would have been more convincing if his voice hadn't been shaking.

"Don't listen to him!" Denise shouted. "It's the Illusionist!"

Mr. Hornsberry cleared his throat. "Actually, it's the Merchant of Emo—"

But Denise cut him off as she started toward the creature. "You're supposed to be dead. We destroyed you in the Sea of Mirrors!"

The Merchant turned from the crowd to face Denny. "The Denise did not destroy me. The Denise destroyed my awful sister—the Illusionist."

"She was your sister?" Denny asked suspiciously.

The Merchant bowed his head, pretending to be embarrassed. "Alas and alack, the Illusionist was the black sheep of the family. And though the Illusionist's loss caused us great pain, we all knew it was for the best." He took a deep breath, forcing his beak to tremble slightly. "And for that, for that we thank the Denise."

Samson buzzed Denise a few times as a warning, but she didn't need anyone to tell her to be careful. "Why are you here?" she demanded. "What do you want?"

"I am the Denise's servant. The Denise summoned me here. What does the *Denise* want?"

"Me?"

"The great Denise summoned me with her wondrous Tablet." The way his voice quivered with desire when he said the Tablet did little to relieve Denny's suspicions.

The father spoke again. "Look, Mr., uh . . ."

"Merchant," the creature answered as he turned back to the crowd. "Just call me the Merchant."

"Well, Mr. Merchant. The point is, Denise here has made our lives unbearable and—"

"Unlivable!" another shouted.

"That's right," others agreed. "We have to stop her! She is evil. Evil!" Once again their anger grew. Once again they started chanting, "Get the Tablet! Get the Tablet! Evil! Evil!"

They started toward her.

But they'd taken only a few steps before the Merchant came to Denny's rescue. He adjusted the setting on his handy-dandy Emotion Generator to MAX. "I think it's time we all loosen up a little," he chortled as he flipped the switch labeled LAUGHTER. A fine mist shot out over half of the crowd. Suddenly they broke into uncontrollable laughter. Back-slapping, hold-your-sides, tears-running-down-your-face laughter. Many dropped to their knees, trying to catch their breath, but it did little good. No one could stop.

Denise and the others stared in amazement. But not for long. The Merchant turned to the other half of the crowd and flipped another switch labeled PEACE.

Another cloud of mist shot out and covered them. Slowly they broke into dreamy smiles. They closed their eyes and sat down on the sand. Why bother standing? There was no need to stand. In fact, there was no need to move. They were feeling so good there was no need to do anything.

Then, for added measure, he turned and gave Samson and Mr. Hornsberry a little squirt as well.

"Sammy! Mr. Hornsberry!"

They also melted into mindless smiles. In a matter of seconds they were also sitting on the ground.

"What have you done?" Denise demanded.

"Your humble servant has done nothing. The Denise is the one who invited me. The Denise is the one who commanded that all the Upside-Downers must feel good."

Denny glanced down at the Tablet. It was true, the words F-E-E-L   G-O-O-D were there as bold as ever. She looked back to the crowd of laughers. By now they were all on the ground holding their sides, gasping for air.

"How . . . how long will this last?"

"The Denise wants Upside-Downers to feel good, doesn't she?"

"Yes, but how—"

"Then the Upside-Downers will feel good."

"But when will it wear off?"

"I'm afraid the effects are permanent."

Permanent! The word hit Denny like a punch in the stomach. "But . . . they can't get up. They can't go anywhere."

"Oh, the Upside-Downers will never go anywhere. The Upside-Downers will never move. The Upside-

Downers will never do anything."

"But . . . but they have to eat. They have to—"

The Merchant shook his head. "The Upside-Downers don't have to do anything ever again. If the Upside-Downers always feel good, why should they?"

"You mean they'll just—"

"Stay here forever," the Merchant nodded. "That is correct."

"But they'll starve to death."

"Oh no. The Denise has destroyed death, remember?"

"So they'll just stay here until they . . . shrivel up for lack of food?"

"Or water," the Merchant agreed. "I'm afraid they'll stay here until they turn to dust and blow away."

"But . . . you just can't—"

"I have no choice," the Merchant sighed. "The Denise wrote it on the Tablet."

Denny turned to the other half of the crowd—the ones with the silly grins on their faces. "You can't sit here!" she yelled. "You got to do something!"

No one spoke.

"Mr. Hornsberry! Samson! Do something!"

No answers. Only smiles.

Panic seized her. She spun to the father who had tried to be the hero. "What about you? What about your daughter! Your family!"

The man said nothing. Why should he? He was feeling too good.

She raced back to the laughers. She knelt to the young man who'd complained about the radio station. "What about you? You can't sit here forever! Don't you want to do something—be something?!"

The boy only laughed harder and louder.

Slowly, unsteadily, Denise rose to her feet.

"I'm afraid the Denise has made quite a mess with that Tablet," the Merchant sighed sadly.

Denny looked around. He was right. What *had* she done? She was supposed to make things better. She was supposed to help their lives, not ruin them. But now . . . now the people were not only twisted and crippled or crazy and out of control . . . now they were laughing insanely and smiling mindlessly. Denny had wanted to make a dream world; instead, she'd created a nightmare.

Angrily she brushed away the tears trying to form in her eyes. "What am I supposed to do?" she demanded. "How can I make it better?"

"Perhaps . . ." The Merchant looked down to the ground and pretended to shrug in humility. "No, that would never work."

"What?"

"It's just . . . well, if the Tablet were turned over to someone more experienced . . ."

Denise looked at him.

"After all," he continued, "the Denise was right, Imager should not be in charge. The Denise tried to do the right thing. The Denise just didn't have the experience."

"And you do?"

The Merchant could see she wasn't completely buying his story, so he changed tactics. All he needed was to get his claws on that Tablet for a minute. That's all it would take to destroy Denny, to annihilate the Upside-Downers and break Imager's heart forever.

"I cannot do it on my own," he shrugged, looking back to the ground. "But together—the Denise with her great understanding of Upside-Downers and I with my superior experience—together we could make this the perfect world the Denise dreamed it would be."

"And . . ." Denise threw another look to the crowd, "all this would stop?"

"Not only will it stop, it will be better, a thousand times better."

Denny looked back to the Tablet. "But how will I know?"

Again the Merchant tried to smile. "I guess the Denise will just have to trust me."

How? How could she trust him? Look what he did to these people—turning them into mindless zombies, crazy laughers. And yet, he was only following orders . . . *her* orders. It really wasn't his fault . . . it was *HERS*.

The Merchant stepped closer. "The Denise should not give up power," he smiled, "just share it. I will make no decision without the Denise. I give the Denise my word."

Denny felt herself weakening. It wasn't as if she were giving up control—just sharing it; they'd be partners. "You promise?" she asked.

"Cross my hearts and hope to die." Again he smiled. "Please, just let me touch it. The Denise may hold it, only allow me to touch it."

"And things will be better?"

"Things will be fantastic. Please . . . for the good of the people."

Denise looked back to the crowd of howling laughers and mindless smilers—a crowd that would remain that way forever.

"For them . . ." the Merchant said very slowly, looking very, very sincere.

Finally, slowly, Denise stretched out the Tablet. Then just as the Merchant's claws touched the stone . . .

Beep . . .
Bop . . .
Burp . . .
Bleep . . .

they were joined by Joshua and Nathan. Oh, and one other traveler . . . TeeBolt.

As Denise turned to see her two friends, the Merchant took advantage of the distraction and ripped the Tablet from her hands. But the possession didn't last long. For when TeeBolt saw his beloved master, he did what any loyal and faithful pet would do. He ran at him full speed.

"No, TeeBolt! Nooo!"

But love knows no bounds. Before the Merchant could stop him, TeeBolt leaped on his master with his front paws (all four of them) and sent them crashing to the ground—TeeBolt, the Merchant, and the Tablet. As they hit the sand, the stone jarred from his hands.

"Get it!" Josh yelled. "Don't let him have the Tablet!"

The Merchant struggled toward it. Not an easy task with a six-hundred-pound pooch on your chest. "Get off me, you nincompoop! Get off me!" But the sound of the Merchant's voice only caused TeeBolt more joy, making him pant harder, drool sloppier, and lick wetter. "No, boy (cough, gag, gag); easy, fella, easy . . ."

Denise raced for the Tablet, but the Merchant was nearly there.

"Grab it!" Nathan cried. "GRAB IT!"

Denny leaped forward. Her hands were stretched out for it. Unfortunately, so were the Merchant's claws.

— CHAPTER ELEVEN —

GREED

Denise and the Merchant rolled back and forth in the sand fighting for the Tablet.

"Let me have it!"

"It's mine!"

"The Denise doesn't know how to—"

With a final pull Denny snatched it from his claws.

"The Denise must give it to—"

She started scratching in the letters, M-I—

"The Denise must give it to me!" He wrapped his claws around it, and with a mighty tug ripped it from her hands—just as she finished the word . . .

M-I-N-E.

Suddenly the Tablet flashed white hot.

"OW!" the Merchant screamed, dropping it to the sand. But when Denny scooped it up, it was as cool as always. The last word she'd written made it clear the

Tablet would always be hers. Always. Nobody else would even be able to touch it.

"All right!" Nathan shouted.

"Nice work!" Josh cried.

"We'll see about *nice*," the Merchant sneered as he rose to his feet and smoothed his ruffled scales. "So the Denise doesn't want to share, does she? Fine. If the Denise wants to be greedy, let her be greedy." He reached to his Emotion Generator and flipped another switch.

"DENNY, LOOK OUT!"

But Nathan was too late. Before Denise could respond, a mist of emotion shot from the Merchant's Generator and covered her entire body.

Denny's eyes grew wide with desire. She pointed to the first thing she saw—a nearby beach umbrella. "Mine!" she cried. As if it caught a mighty wind, the umbrella ripped from the sand and flew across the beach to Denise. It landed on the ground beside her— the first of many possessions.

Josh and Nate looked on with astonishment.

She pointed at the next thing she saw—a lifeguard station. "Mine!" she cried. Immediately it was at her side. A little tipsy from the sudden move, but there, nonetheless.

The Merchant started to laugh. "If the Denise wants to control the Tablet, let her. I'll simply control the Denise."

"Mine!" Denise pointed at a pair of sandals on the feet of one of the laughers. A moment later they were on Denny's feet.

"You can't control her!" Josh cried.

"Hasn't the Joshua learned yet?" the Merchant laughed. "Whoever controls the emotions controls the person."

"We'll see about that," Josh said, reaching for his waterskin. "You may have her now, but not for long."

"Oh yes, very long. And I'll soon have the Joshua and the Nathan as well."

"No way," Nathan declared, raising his shield and stepping forward. The armor fit much better now. Almost perfect. "With this shield and that water you can't touch us."

"The Nathan has a point. *I* can't." He turned to Denise and spoke. "Look at the Nathan's nice shiny armor. Wouldn't the Denise love to have that?"

Denise smiled and pointed. "Mine!"

Immediately the shield was ripped away and the armor torn off. Nathan stood only in his T-shirt and jeans.

"Denny!" he cried. But she did not hear him over the Merchant's laughter.

Now the brothers were defenseless. They still had the water, but there wasn't a shred of protection from the emotions.

"Let's see," the Merchant mused as he looked over the switches strapped to his chest. "What will it be. FEAR, TERROR? No, no . . . we tried that before. An interesting reaction, but not quite the effect we're looking for."

"Listen . . ." Joshua tried to reason.

But the Merchant wasn't listening. "Ah, here's a nice one."

" . . . you just can't go around—"

"How about a little HOPELESSNESS?"

"A little what?"

"HOPELESSNESS . . . It's one of my favorites— and soon to be yours."

"No, please . . . please . . ." Nathan begged.

He flipped the switch.

The brothers watched helplessly as the mist shot from the Generator and gently rained down upon them.

"Listro Q!" Aristophenix shouted over the alarms in Master Control.

Listro Q turned to his partner. No words had to be said. They both knew what needed to be done. The tall purple creature reached into his pocket for another Cross-Dimensionalizer.

"Hold it," the Weaver interrupted. "It's too dangerous."

"Other choice, what do we have?" Listro Q asked.

"There's no way of knowing the outcome," the Weaver warned. "The tapestries are completely unraveled, yes they are."

"If don't go we," Listro Q quietly stated, "then our friends destroyed will be?"

Aristophenix continued:

Not only our friends,
but all Upside-Downers as well.
We must stop the Merchant
from casting his spell.

"You don't understand," the Weaver insisted. "There is nothing I can do if you fall under his power."

Aristophenix nodded.

We know the risks,
our chances are few.
But they're Imager's beloved,
what more can we do?

The Weaver took a deep breath. It was true. The

Upside-down Kingdom was Imager's favorite. No price was too great to save them. Imager proved that by his own sacrifice many epochs earlier. And if Imager was willing to pay such a price, how could he, the Weaver, prevent Listro Q and Aristophenix from doing any less?

The two quietly waited for his decision.

At last he nodded . . . slowly, sadly.

Listro Q entered the quadrants as Aristophenix fired off one last poem:

> Don't worry 'bout us,
> we're pros, don't ya know.
> Them quadrants they're a entered,
> so let's get on with the—

Beep . . .
Bop . . .
Burp . . .
Bleep . . .

and they were gone.

The Weaver stood alone. He could feel the lump growing in his throat, the moisture burning in his eyes. Finally he turned back to the screen. "I'm going to miss those poems," he whispered hoarsely to himself, "yes, I am."

CHAPTER TWELVE

TO THE RESCUE
...SORT OF

By the time Aristophenix and Listro Q arrived in the Upside-down Kingdom, the situation was hopeless . . . literally. The Merchant had fired the mist over the boys and now they felt completely HOPELESS.

"Oh, hello," Nathan greeted them flatly. "Sorry you had to come all this way just to get destroyed."

"Say you what?" Listro Q asked in surprise.

"He's got us," Joshua explained. "The Merchant's too powerful for us to win."

"Well, TeeBolt, looky here," the Merchant clucked to his panting pet. "More victims. Let's see . . ." He looked down to his switches. "What would be an appropriate emotion for nosy, do-gooder Fayrahnians?"

Aristophenix shot a nervous look to the Merchant, then back to the boys. There wasn't much time. He tried to explain:

Them are only emotions,
over you that he's tossed.
Don't let 'em control you,
Ya can still be yer boss.

"It's no use," Joshua sighed.

"It's hopeless," Nathan agreed. "They've got all my armor. There's no way we can defend ourselves."

The Merchant continued surveying his emotion switches. He was in no hurry. "Let's see, we have ANGER, ANXIOUSNESS, APATHY . . ."

Aristophenix tried again:

Don't go by your feelings,
go by what you know.
Trust Imager's promise
that you'll overthrow this here foe.

"I don't see how," Josh sighed.

"It's hopeless," Nathan repeated.

"BASHFUL, BEWILDERED, BITTER . . ."

Aristophenix turned to Listro Q. Neither had an idea. Not a clue where to start. If the boys refused to believe, how could they force them?

Then there was the little matter of the Merchant and his Generator. "FOOLISH, FRANTIC, FRIENDLY . . ."

Should they just grab Samson and hightail it back to Fayrah before they got zapped? After all, they didn't create these problems, Denny did. As an Upside-Downer it was *her* choice—her decision.

And yet, Imager had such love for these people. Come to think of it, so did Aristophenix and Listro Q. Throughout their journeys together a deep friendship had grown. A friendship so strong that they couldn't leave the kids—even if it was their fault. No, Aristo-

phenix and Listro Q had to stay. They had to stay and
. . . and . . . And what?

Suddenly Listro Q's eyes lit up. He stepped toward
Joshua. "Water still you have in waterskin?"

"Sure, but look how torn it is," Joshua complained.
"Everything's ruined. Nothing's going right. The Merchant's got Nathan's shield, he's controlling Denny,
you're about to get zapped, everything's just hope—"

"Best defense, offense is," Listro Q said as he
grabbed the waterskin.

"OPTIMISTIC, OUT-OF-IT, OUTRAGE . . . That's
it!" The Merchant grinned. "OUTRAGE would be
nice." He reached to the switch. "OUTRAGE would be
very nice."

Aristophenix quickly whispered to Listro Q:

I don't know what you're planning,
but it better be quick.
Cuz we got 2.8 seconds
'fore he switches that switch.

Listro Q unfolded the gash in the top of the waterskin.

"Put that away!" the Merchant shouted. "Put that
away this instant!"

"What are you doing?" Josh cried. "You're gonna
make him madder—he'll make things worse!"

"Listen," Listro Q commanded, "very carefully listen."

"To what?"

But Listro Q didn't answer. Instead, he lifted the
waterskin over Joshua's head and poured the liquid
words and letters over him.

"Stop it!" the Merchant shouted.

Next, he spun around and poured some over Nathan's head.

"Stop it!" the Merchant cried. He'd had enough. He quickly flipped the switch and fired OUTRAGE . . . but not before Aristophenix cried out to the brothers:

Trust in Imager's words,
what you hear is the truth.
Feelings are fickle,
but his words are absolu—

That was as far as he got. The emotion covered Listro Q and Aristophenix.

"What are you talking about?" Joshua whined. "What words?"

"Why do I have to explain everything for you!" Aristophenix snapped. "Use your brain for once!"

"At them don't shout!" Listro Q yelled. He was equally as outraged.

Aristophenix turned on his friend and shouted back, "Don't tell me what to do you, you . . . purple, pretentious . . . pinhead!"

Listro Q pulled up his sleeves. "Who are you calling purple!?"

The Merchant roared with laughter. "So much for Fayrahnian love!" But he didn't laugh long.

"Listen!" Josh cried. "What is that?"

"I don't hear anything," Nate whined.

"Shhh . . ."

Nathan strained to hear. "It's nothing. Just the wind blowing in the—wait a minute. It, it sounds like . . . is that somebody whispering?"

The Merchant glanced nervously around. "I don't hear anything. What are you talking about?"

Josh turned to his brother. "Can you make it out?"

Nathan shook his head.

Both boys continued to strain. The words were

very quiet. Very small. But they were very, very persistent.

"You will defeat him."
"You will defeat him."

"I still can't—"
"Shhh!"

"You will defeat him."
"You will defeat him."
"You will defeat him."

"Can you make it out now?"
"Almost . . ."

"You Will Defeat Him."
"You Will Defeat Him."

Nathan's eyes widened. He'd heard that voice once before. Once when Denny was trapped in the Experiment. "Is that. . . ?"

Josh nodded. "Imager. That's what he said when we were at the Center. Those were his words!"

"I hear nothing!" the Merchant scorned.

The voice continued:

"You will defeat him."
"YOU WILL DEFEAT HIM."
"YOU WILL DEFEAT HIM."

"It's in the water!" Nathan exclaimed. He touched the liquid still dripping from his face. "His voice is in the water!"

"YOU WILL DEFEAT HIM."
"YOU WILL DEFEAT HIM."

"Of course it's in the water," Aristophenix angrily shouted. "It's his words!"

"But it's hopeless!" Joshua insisted. "We can't defeat him!"

"That's right," Nathan whined. "It's hopeless."

"Exactly," the Merchant sneered. "Trust your feelings. They are truth. Listen to your feelings, not these words."

The brothers looked to the Merchant. As they looked and listened to him, their feeling of HOPE-LESSNESS grew stronger. And as the HOPELESS-NESS grew stronger, the still small voice of the water grew weaker. . . .

"YOU WILL DEFEAT HIM."
"You Will Defeat Him."
"You will defeat him."

"Why is it fading?" Joshua cried.

It was Listro Q's turn to explode with anger. "Fading his voice is not! Your hearing, that is what's fading!"

"What?"

"If trust Imager's words, then power of feelings will fade! But if trust power of feelings, then Imager's words will fade!"

"That's right," Aristophenix snapped:

The decision is yours
who you'll follow today.
Either Imager's words,
or your feelings obey.

"Imager's words—" Joshua shouted. "I want to follow Imager's words but—"

Suddenly the voice grew louder:

"You Will Defeat Him."
"YOU WILL DEFEAT HIM."

"But I *feel* so helpless."

Immediately the voice started to fade.

"No, Josh!" Nathan cried. "We have to trust his

words. His words are what's true!"

"YOU WILL DEFEAT HIM."
"YOU WILL DEFEAT HIM."
"YOU WILL DEFEAT HIM."

"But it's ... it's so hard," Josh complained. "I can't."

Again the words started to fade.

"I know," Nathan cried, "but remember ... remember how they helped us in the Sea of Mirrors? How they saved your life?"

"Yes," Josh nodded.

"Or how they saved me from Bobok's Menagerie?"

"Yes."

But that was as far as Nathan got. "STOP IT!" the Merchant shouted as he fired another shot of HOPE-LESSNESS at him.

The mist covered Nathan. It was Joshua's turn to pick up the ball. "How 'bout the way Imager saved Denny from the Experiment."

"Yes," Nathan, groaned. "And me from Seerlo!"

"You Will Defeat Him."
"YOU WILL DEFEAT HIM."

"It's working, Nathan! Keep remembering what he did!"

"Fools!" the Merchant shouted. "Your feelings are now! Trust your feelings, not some long and forgotten—"

"How 'bout his power to reweave Denny?" Nathan gasped.

"Or to destroy Keygarp!"

"And Seerlo!" Nathan shouted.

"YOU WILL DEFEAT HIM."

"YOU WILL DEFEAT HIM."
"YOU WILL DEFEAT HIM."

"Stop it! Stop it at once! Imager is nothing! His promises are noth—"

"NO!" Josh cried, spinning around to face him. "*YOU* ARE NOTHING! *YOU* WILL BE DEFEATED!"

"You are a fool!" the Merchant moved in for the kill. "Prove to me these things are real—"

"Prove?"

"You're the scientist! Can you touch those memories? . . . can you prove them?"

"Well . . . no," Josh started to falter. "They're just memories, there's no—"

"WE WILL DEFEAT YOU!" Nathan barged in. "JOSHUA AND I WILL DEFEAT YOU! RIGHT, JOSH?"

Josh was still trying to recover from the last blow.

"RIGHT, JOSH!"

Joshua looked to his brother. The little guy's eyes were full of confidence. But it was a fragile kind of confidence. Like Josh, he was barely hanging on. Neither boy could beat the Merchant on their own. That was obvious. But as they combined forces, as they combined what little faith they had, as they helped each other remember Imager's deeds . . .

"That's right!" Josh forced himself to shout. "His words have never failed!"

"YOU WILL DEFEAT HIM."
"YOU WILL DEFEAT HIM."
"YOU WILL DEFEAT HIM."

"They destroyed the Illusionist!" Nathan yelled. "That's right!"

"They destroyed Bobok!"

"That's right!"

"They destroyed Seerlo!"

Finally Josh was able to turn on the Merchant. "And they'll destroy you!"

The words were louder now than ever:

"YOU WILL DEFEAT HIM."
"YOU WILL DEFEAT HIM."
"YOU WILL DEFEAT HIM."

With growing confidence Joshua turned to Listro Q and reached for the waterskin.

"What are you doing?" the Merchant demanded.

Josh unfolded the gash at the top of the waterskin and started toward the Merchant.

"Stay away! Stay away!" the Merchant ordered.

Joshua paid little attention. Instead, he and Nathan continued forward.

The Merchant backed away. "I'm warning you. Stay away with that!"

The boys closed in.

In desperation the Merchant turned to his faithful companion. "TeeBolt—TeeBolt, attack!"

But TeeBolt was doing what he did best—running for his life in the opposite direction.

Now the Merchant was only a few feet away. Now it was time to send him back home. Joshua held out the waterskin. "I think it's time for you to go."

"But I like it here," the Merchant hissed. Before Joshua could stop him, he fired off another volley of HOPELESSNESS. And another. And another.

Both boys staggered under the impact.

"There's plenty more where this came from!" the

Merchant roared with confidence.

Imager's voice quickly started to fade.

"JOSH!" Nathan shouted. "MORE WATER! WE NEED MORE WATER!"

Josh raised the waterskin and poured it over his head.

The voice grew louder.

He tossed the skin to Nathan who followed suit.

The Merchant was in a panic. He twirled to Denny. "The Denise . . . the Denise must do something! The Denise must write—"

But Denise already had her plan. She had been watching long enough. Still consumed with GREED, she knew exactly what she wanted. She pointed to the water in Josh's waterskin. "Want!"

Immediately all of the water was sucked from the skin and dumped onto Denny. From head to toe the liquid words and letters washed over her. She coughed and gasped, trying to catch her breath.

And for the first time she also heard Imager's voice. Loud and clear.

"YOU WILL DEFEAT HIM."
"YOU WILL DEFEAT HIM."
"YOU WILL DEFEAT HIM."

"Listen to his words!" Joshua shouted. "Trust his words. Trust his words, not your feelings!"

But Denny could barely hear him above the Merchant's shrieking. "DON'T BELIEVE THEM! I CAN GIVE YOU ANYTHING YOU WANT. JUST NAME IT. WE'RE PARTNERS, REMEMBER?"

Denise nodded.

"NO, DENNY!" Josh cried. "NO!"

The Merchant grinned.

"DENNY! DON'T!" Nathan pleaded. "DON'T TRUST HIM! LISTEN TO THE WORDS!"

Slowly Denise raised her hand and started to point. The Merchant's grin broadened. "Anything, my dear . . . anything at all!"

"DENNY—NO!" Nathan raced toward her, but Josh grabbed him and held him back.

"Let me go, let me go!"

"It won't do any good, Nate—she has to decide!"

Josh was right. The struggle ceased. Both boys watched as Denny opened her mouth. She spoke only three words. "That . . ." she said, pointing at the Emotion Generator. "I want!"

Immediately the Generator was ripped from the Merchant's chest and resting in her hands.

"GIVE THAT BACK! GIVE THAT BACK TO ME!"

"ALL RIGHT, DENNY!" the boys shouted. "WAY TO GO!"

"GIVE THAT BACK TO ME, NOW!" The Merchant started toward her but hesitated as he saw that she was still dripping with Imager's water. "GIVE IT TO ME!"

"I'm sorry." Denise seemed almost apologetic. "I can't give you this, but I might have something else." She looked down to the Generator in her hands and scanned the rows of silver switches.

"What are you doing?" The Merchant started to back up. "Put that down! You don't know how to use it!"

Denny spotted a switch and smiled slightly. She pointed the Generator toward the Merchant.

"The Denise doesn't know what she's doing. The Denise doesn't—"

She fired and a jet of mist shot out.

"NOOOOO. . . !"

It fell gently over the Merchant.

"NO!" he screamed. "NO! NO! NO!" He began running and whimpering in tight little circles. "NO, I DO NOT FEEL THIS! I DO NOT FEEL THIS! NO! NO! NO! NO!!!"

The boys looked on in wonder as the Merchant continued to shriek in agony. Finally he unfurled his leathery wings.

"How 'bout one for the road?" Denise asked as she fired off another volley.

"NOOOO!!!" he screamed. "NO! NO! NO! NO!" He flapped his wings and rose quickly into the air. "NO! NO! NO!" Then, with several more thrusts, he disappeared into the sky, racing toward deepest space. Only the echoes of his protest remained behind. "NO, No, no, nooo . . ."

"Denny!" The boys raced to her and threw their arms around her.

"Come on, guys," she coughed, "knock it off. I can't breathe, I can't breathe."

But the brothers never let her have her way before, why should they start now? They just kept hugging her for all they were worth. Finally they separated. "You OK?" they asked. "Sure you're feeling all right now?"

"*Feelings?*" she grinned. "If it's OK with you, I wouldn't put too much trust in *feelings*, all right?"

All three broke out laughing. It had been the first time they'd laughed in quite a while. And it felt good. Very good.

"But what did you zap him with?" Nathan asked. "What type of emotion could cause him so much pain?"

"Oh, that's easy," Denise grinned. "I got him with the one he hated most."

"Yeah . . . which is . . ."

"I nailed him with . . . LOVE."

CHAPTER THIRTEEN

ANOTHER DAY, ANOTHER SAVED PLANET

It didn't take long for Denny to get things back to normal. After all, she still had the Tablet—she was still the boss.

With a few strokes of her trusty pen everyone began feeling their normal emotions. Mr. Hornsberry was particularly grateful since it's tough to be a snob when you're sitting on the ground grinning like a fool. Aristophenix and Listro Q were also thankful. They were getting a little tired of shouting and yelling at everyone. And Samson? Samson was back to his usual sassy self. Which meant he didn't hesitate to dive-bomb Denny a number of times and give her a good piece of his mind. A real good piece.

"Here," Denise sighed as she handed Aristophenix the Merchant's Generator of Emotions. "Do whatever you need to get rid of this thing, will you?"

I'll dispose of it quickly,
on that you can depend.
As of now the Merchant's power
is officially at an end.

"I tell you," Nathan spoke up, "if I never feel another emotion, it will be too soon."

Listro Q shook his head in disagreement. "Emotions, good they are, to help us experience life."

"He's right," Aristophenix insisted:

Emotions are good,
'cause they help us to deal
with life's ups and downs.
It's swell that we feel.

Listro Q nodded. "Like instruments on dashboard. Emotions tell us what is happening inside."

"What are you talking about?" Nathan asked.

Joshua thought he understood. "You're saying emotions are like gauges that help us know what's going on inside us?"

"Gauges and thermometers of your mind, yes they are."

"We just have to make sure we're controlling them and they're not controlling us," Josh offered.

"Correct you are."

"Excuse me . . . excuse me, please?" It was the father of the candy-bar eater. Behind him stood the hundreds of people who had been on the ground laughing and smiling. Their uncontrollable emotions were now under control, but many of their bodies were still ravaged beyond belief. "There's a lot more that has to be done," he said, motioning to the crowd. "We still need your help."

Denise turned to the throng. He was right. Things

were still quite a mess. She took a deep breath and sighed. "Where do I begin?"

"All things make, as they used to be," Listro Q offered.

"You mean like Imager had before I fixed them?"

Josh grinned. "Now there's an idea!"

A gentle murmur of approval swept through the crowd.

"But how? I mean, if I give them back pain, they'll all suffer. If I give them death, lots of them will die. And what about all those rules I took away. . . ?" She let out another heavy sigh and looked down at the Tablet. "I tell you, it would be better if I'd never even found this thing."

"Precisely," Listro Q grinned.

"What?"

"That very thing you can make happen."

"You're not serious?"

Aristophenix agreed:

None of this would be
if the Tablet never was.
So write, "It never existed,"
and see what it does.

"But then," Denise protested, "then I won't have the power to make things happen."

"Correct you are," Listro Q said. "Then rely only on Imager you must."

"But . . ."

"Live by his plan, your only option."

"But—"

Either you trust him or don't,
the decision is plain.
Either Imager's the boss,
or this insane life remains.

Denise turned back to the crowd. Things *were* insane. He was right about that. She'd only made a few little changes, written a few little words, and look what happened. She had tried to help these people. Instead, she had nearly destroyed them. Instead of perfect people, she had turned them into out-of-control monsters. Monsters who now stood silently, pleading for her help, waiting for her decision.

Denny hated the thought of losing control. But worse, she hated the thought of keeping it. It's true, there were thousands of things she didn't understand about Imager's ways. She probably never would. But she did know one thing. He did seem to know what he was doing.

Finally she reached into her pocket and pulled out the felt pen. "Well, it's been real," she grinned.

"Too real," Josh grinned back.

The others chuckled nervously as they waited in anticipation.

"See ya around," she said to the Tablet as she raised her pen and wrote the words . . .

Y-O-U D-O-N-'T E-X-I-S-T

———————

Denise woke with a start. For a minute she didn't know where she was—that is, until she felt the jab of a steel armrest in her ribs, then the sticky vinyl against her arms, and finally the cramp in her neck.

Ah, yes, the hospital chair.

She looked over at her mother, who was still asleep—the sedative was still working. In fact, in the dim morning light her mother looked peaceful, almost happy.

But something had changed. For some reason Denny's anger about her mom was gone. She wasn't sure why. Maybe it had something to do with the strange dream she'd just had. Talk about weird.

There was a gentle tapping at the door.

Denny rose from the chair, crossed to the door and opened it. "Josh, Nathan . . ."

"Sorry we couldn't come last night," Josh whispered as they stepped inside. "We had to watch Grandpa's store."

"How's she doing?" Nathan asked as he limped past Denise to look at her mom.

"Pretty good," Denny said as she turned to watch her sleep.

"You stay here all night?" Josh asked.

"Yeah," Denise said, rubbing her stiff neck. "It wasn't too bad. Except for the dream . . . talk about weird."

The boys exchanged nervous glances.

"The dream?" Josh asked.

"Yeah . . . it was all about this flat stone, and me writing on it, and—"

"Was there a creature in it?" Josh asked. "Some guy with a machine strapped to his chest?"

"Well . . . yeah. How did—"

"And a six-legged dog?" Nate continued.

"How'd you guys know?"

Again the boys looked to each other. Josh finally cleared his throat. "Nathan had the same dream."

"What??"

He continued. "So did I."

"You're kidding me!"

Denny's mother stirred slightly at the outburst.

"Last night," Nathan whispered.

"You mean we all three dreamed the same dream?!"

"About a Tablet . . ."

Denny nodded. "And some creep trying to take over the world."

"And you ruling instead of Imager."

Denise leaned against the wall to steady herself. On the weirdness scale this was . . . well, it was *off* the scale. "How?" she asked. "Why?"

No one had an answer.

Then she asked another question, the one they were all thinking. "This probably has something to do with the Fayrahnians, doesn't it?"

"Probably," Josh answered. "Next time we see them, we're gonna have to ask."

"You bet we are," Nathan agreed.

Denny nodded quietly to herself. "We sure are. . . ."

———

Meanwhile, somewhere between the Upside-down Kingdom and Fayrah, roly-poly Aristophenix, purple Listro Q, and the feisty Samson were cross-dimensionalizing home.

"So bits and pieces, only they'll remember?" Listro Q thought to Aristophenix.

Aristophenix nodded:

A foggy dream
is all they'll recall.
Though it will help in their growth
as they give Imager all.

Aristophenix folded his arms in satisfaction. As the leader of the group, he was pretty pleased with the way he'd pulled things off. Actually, real pleased.

Actually, he was about to burst with pride.

"Only one question to ask have I," Listro Q thought.

"Ask away, my good man," Aristophenix thought back confidently, *"ask away."*

"If normal, everything back is to . . ."

"Yes . . ."

"Then," Listro Q continued while pointing just past Aristophenix, *"why a new companion have we?"*

"What new companion?" Aristophenix thought as he turned. *"We don't have a new—"*

Suddenly he was hit by a galloping six-legged dog. Before he could be stopped, the grateful animal hopped on his chest and began slurping and licking and drooling.

"Easy fella! Down boy . . ."

Samson and Listro Q began to laugh.

"Come on, fella . . . easy now . . . somebody call him off, call him off!"

His buddies struggled to pull the animal away, but it did no good. (Not that they tried all that hard.) It looked as if TeeBolt had found a new master. And he would remain glued to his side (drool and all) for a long, long time.